THE NOCTURNALS

Book Two
The Ominous Eye

Tracey Hecht

Fabled Films Press
New York

Published by Fabled Films LLC, New York

ISBN: 978-1-944020-10-1

Library of Congress Control Number 2016944966

First Paperback Edition: July 2017

13 5 7 9 10 8 6 4 2

Cover Designed by Jaime Mendola-Hobbie
Jacket Art by Kate Liebman
Interior Book Design by Notion Studio
Typeset in Stemple Garamond, Mrs. Ant and Pacific Northwest
Printed by Everbest in China

FABLED FILMS PRESS
NEW YORK CITY
www.fabledfilms.com

For information on bulk purchases for promotional use please contact Consortium Book Sales & Distribution Sales department at Sales.Orders@cbsd.com or 1-800-283-3572

From the paws of
Sarah Fieber.
For her mom
But not without Tracey, Tommy, and Rumur.

Book Two
The Ominous Eye

To see a map of the Brigade's adventure,
visit www.nocturnalsworld.com/map/

Chapter One
BOOM!

"Really, *amigo*? Another one?" Bismark glided down from his pomelo tree and plopped next to his friend Tobin. It was a small plop, because Bismark was a sugar glider, a tiny marsupial much like a flying squirrel. "If you keep stuffing yourself like a warthog, I'm afraid you might explode!"

Tobin froze, termite in claw, and glanced at his belly. It was the only part of the pangolin's anteater-like body not covered in hard, brown scales…and it was grumbling loudly. "Just one more," he said, smiling bashfully.

Tobin opened his mouth and unrolled his long, thin tongue. It was so long, in fact, that it had to be coiled and stored in his stomach. But when it was time to eat—like now—he unfurled it like a long, pink vine.

The pangolin grinned at the fat, wriggly insect. This termite was going to be a good one.

But then a strange noise startled him. "Oh goodness!" Tobin exclaimed. At once, he shot his tongue into his belly, snapped his jaw shut, and curled into a ball. It was the position he took when he became frightened, which happened often and easily. "Did you hear that?" He stared into the darkness. "I heard a faint sort of rumble!"

"*Mon dieu*," teased the sugar glider. "Don't tell me you're about to blow."

Bismark scrunched his tiny face and plugged his nose. When the pangolin got really scared, he sometimes released a smell from his scent glands that was so stinky, it could knock an angry rhinoceros out cold.

"Oh goodness, Bismark! It's not that," Tobin said. He peeked through his claws at the leaves of the tree overhead. They were moving, but he could not feel any wind. "Listen!"

Boom!

Bismark sighed and cupped his tiny ear with one paw. "I *do* hear something…" he mused. The sugar glider thoughtfully stroked his chin as he tried to identify the strange vibration. Then, suddenly, he pumped his small fist in the air. "Eureka!" he cried. "But of course! It's the beating of my true love's heart. My ravishing Dawn must be near."

Quickly, the sugar glider licked his paws, smoothed his fur over the bald spot in the center of his scalp, and searched for signs of the fox. She was the leader of the Nocturnal Brigade—the group the three friends had formed to protect the animals of the valley who needed their help. She also happened to be Bismark's not-so-secret love.

Sure enough, Dawn emerged from the brush with a soft patter. Her amber eyes were alert and darted over her surroundings.

"I knew it!" declared Bismark proudly. "And now that I see you and your radiant red fur, *mon amour*, I'm shaken straight to the core."

"Shaken, yes," Dawn said breathlessly.

Slowly, Tobin uncurled and stood up. The rumble grew louder, and he felt a tremor beneath him. The pangolin glanced at the ground. Pebbles jumped at his feet. "The earth! It's moving!"

"My silly *amigo*—that is just what it feels like when my beautiful Dawn comes into view!"

"There's no time for romance," said Dawn. The tawny fur along her back stood up like blades of wild grass. "We need to take cover. These tremors are growing larger."

"Nonsense!" cried Bismark. "The only thing growing is the surge of love in my heart! And it is all for you, my lady!"

Sssssss. A faint hiss rose from the ground.

Bismark let out a high-pitched shriek and leaped onto Dawn's back. "By all that glides! Is that a snake I hear?"

"No," said the fox, "but let's move. We need to find a safe place at once." She pointed uphill, at a boulder with a large hole carved into it. Then she plucked Bismark from her back and bounded toward it, seeking its shelter.

As the trio dashed through the trees toward high ground, the hiss around them turned into a sizzle. Soon, the ground was crackling and popping beneath their paws. Dawn leaped into the hole in the boulder, and Bismark and Tobin followed.

Bismark clutched Dawn's slender leg while Tobin hesitantly peered past the rock's edge.

"Oh no," cried the pangolin. "Look!"

In the distance, a thick veil of steam spiraled through the night air. As the wind picked up speed, the steam billowed toward the three friends. The moon flashed in and out from behind the sheet of white clouds.

Tobin shut his eyes tight, dizzy from the sudden humidity and the rapid changes of light. The scent of rotten eggs filled his sensitive nostrils as the steam spread over the animals and blanketed them in a haze.

The frightened cries of other creatures echoed from beyond the trees. The bushes rustled and shook as animals throughout the valley bolted through the forest in search of safe places to hide. The Brigade, however, held their ground and each other.

Bismark wiped a thick bead of sweat from his brow then fanned himself with the wing-like flaps that connected his arms and legs. "Is it just me," he gasped, "or is it getting hot out here?"

A low hum rang through the air. The pangolin felt his heart shake as the sound grew to a growl, drowning out everything else.

Then, suddenly, all was still. The ground no longer shook. The air no longer rang. The animals, the branches, the leaves — all fell quiet.

"Phew!" exclaimed Bismark. The sugar glider

brushed some loose dirt off his flaps. "What a doozy! That shaking, that groaning, that heat?" He exhaled with great relief. "*Muy caliente*! At least it's over…"

BOOM!

A giant blast shook the earth. The ground rocked and the wind roared and the three animals grasped one another in terror. A giant column of smoke rose up from the distant hills. And then, all went black.

Chapter Two
THE CRATER

"Tobin? Bismark? Where are you?" Dawn struggled to see through the darkness.

A cloud of ash hung in the air, blotting out the light from the stars. Slowly, the ash began to fall, carpeting the ground in a soft layer of gray.

"Oh goodness, I'm right here!" called the pangolin, shuffling toward the sound of Dawn's voice.

Bismark appeared from under a small pile of cinders. "*Mon dieu!*" he cried. "What was that rumble, that thunder, that bang?"

"I don't know, but we must find out," Dawn said.

"Are you *loco*, my love?" Bismark coughed. "You want to go *toward* the big boom?"

Dawn stood tall. "Yes," she said. Her ears still rang from the blast, making her voice sound hollow and foreign to her. She lowered her gaze to the ground—it was splintered with zigzagging cracks. "Even this far away, there is damage. Who knows how bad it is near the blast?"

Tobin saw the determined face of his leader. Despite his nerves, he nodded in agreement.

"So be it! Bold in adventure, brave in challenge, the Nocturnal Brigade to the rescue!" cried Bismark. With a flourish, he drew out his glittering, blue snakeskin cape—the costume the Brigade wore when they were on a mission. Dawn and Tobin took their capes out, too, and fastened them around their necks. Within a moment, the trio was ready. It was time to keep the Brigade's promise to protect the animals of the night.

"I think the sound came from that direction," said Dawn. She pointed toward a mountain in the near distance. "Let's go."

The Brigade crept toward the peak. The ground was hot and glowed red with embers. Carefully, the animals plowed their way through the smoldering fields of ash and broken rock.

"Pee-yew!" exclaimed Bismark. "Either Tobin's scared out of his scales, or this stuff smells like rot!"

"Oh goodness, Bismark—you know that's not me!" The pangolin squinted, struggling to keep Dawn in sight. Usually, to help his poor eyesight, he tracked the white tip of her tail. But now it, like everything else, was painted a dull shade of gray. "Oof," he muttered, rubbing his eyes. "I can't even see the moon."

Despite being almost full, the moon was barely a blur, fighting to shine through the clouds of ash. The light that did reach the ground was filtered and flat.

"Everything's so different. Even the air." Tobin coughed. He flicked some ash from his paw. "It feels like another planet."

"A planet of nightmares!" cried Bismark. The sugar glider flapped his way through the dust, attempting to wave it away, but just whipping it into his own face in the process. "What sort of world is this?" he wheezed. "The earth: scorched and lifeless! The air: stinky with fumes! My fur: stripped of its incredible sheen! My eyes: struggling to see my love's face!" He scoffed. "This is no place for me, *mis amigos*. I say we turn back!"

Dawn came to a halt.

"Hmm?" Bismark cocked his head. "Have I convinced you?"

"Everyone, stop," warned the fox. Her voice

was sharp and abrupt. "Do not take another step."

The animals froze. Without their movement stirring the air, some of the ash settled down and the landscape came into view. Right in front of them was the jagged edge of a cliff.

Tobin gazed over the rim and gulped. If not for Dawn, he'd be plummeting over the edge, down, down, down into a deep, dark hole. The pangolin blinked, staring below in disbelief. It looked like a giant angry monster had attacked the earth, leaving a crater as big as a lake.

"Something smashed into the ground," said the fox. But she could not figure out what it possibly could have been. Curious, Dawn stepped toward the gaping hole and curled her paws over its rim. Then she leaned forward for a better look. Her eyes flashed in alarm.

"Dawn?" Tobin's tail coiled in fear. Nevertheless, he crept forward, joining the fox at the edge of the crater. With a deep breath, he followed her gaze into the hole. "Oh goodness!" he gasped.

Bismark's face tightened with frustration. "What could be so interesting that it steals my lovely Dawn's breath? It must be done away with at once!" Bismark flexed his scrawny muscle, examined it with a satisfied nod, then nudged past Tobin's rear. "Please, move aside.

Allow me, animal *extraordinaire*, *macho* marsupial, and your one true love," he said, winking at the fox, "to conquer whatever might—"

But as he peered down into the giant hole, Bismark's already bulbous eyes nearly bulged out of his skull. "Holy glider!" he cried. "I cannot believe what my small but extraordinary peepers see!" His heart pounded inside his small ribcage.

At the bottom of the crater, pressed into the dirt, was the outline of an animal so huge and so fearsome, only one word could describe it—BEAST.

Chapter Three
THE MONSTER'S SHADOW

"Dawn?" Tobin whispered. "What is it?"

The fox opened her mouth to speak, but no words came. What she saw was unlike anything she had seen before.

The creature that had left its mark in the bottom of the crater had the general shape of a lizard, but was hundreds of times larger. Its spine was the length and width of a full-grown tree. Its massive feet could have crushed the three Brigade-mates with ease. A row of sharp-looking spikes ran the length of its back and down its long, whip-like tail. No reptile—not even a full-grown crocodile—was near that enormous.

"It's *n-n-nada*, I'm sure," stuttered Bismark. He wiped beads of sweat from his brow, staining his face with ash. "N-nothing that I cannot c-conquer." The sugar glider stood as tall as he possibly could and raised a trembling fist in the air.

Tobin took a step back. Dawn clenched her jaw. Neither one spoke.

Finally, unable to remain silent, Bismark leaped up, flaps outstretched. "Hello?" he yelped. "*Bonjour?* Someone, anyone? Explain this now!"

Dawn looked down at the sugar glider, but still did not say a word.

Bismark placed his paws on his hips. "Well then," he started, "I shall take charge. I shall explain!" His breath had grown fast, and his chest pulsed with nerves. "You want to know what it is, pangolin?"

Tobin gulped.

"I'll tell you... It's...it's...it's a monster! A monster, I say!" Bismark's eyes flashed with fear.

Edging next to the fox, he gazed down. "Do you see this?" he screeched. "That skull, those spikes, that tail? The size of this hole? A monster, a terrifying monster, destroyed this ground. We are doomed, I tell you! Doomed!"

"Bismark—" Dawn tried to calm the sugar glider, But he was already off on one of his rants.

"I've heard of these creatures before, *mi amor*. Terrorizing the land with their terrible rage! Racing after prey, covering huge distances with a single leap! Blowing smoke and flames at poor little sugar gliders!" Bismark raised a flap to his forehead. "It's a dragon!"

Tobin let out a gasp. Though he'd never actually seen one, he had heard about dragons in myths. And they usually weren't friendly.

"Stop that," said Dawn. The fox glared at the sugar glider. But when she thought about it, she couldn't come up with any other explanation. A huge blast of smoke, a break in the earth, and now this?

Dawn shook her shoulders, trying to think logically. No, she concluded. Dragons were just the invention of storytellers. But as the fox looked again at the enormous black shape down below, her puzzlement returned.

Careful to keep her breath even, she turned toward her friends. "We must warn the animals of the valley," she said, "but let's choose our words wisely. The last thing we want is to frighten everyone. We don't want to create panic."

"Panic?" yelped Bismark. "Panic, you say?" The sugar glider hopped back and forth on his toes and scratched at his bald spot in a frenzy. "No, no, no. No need to panic."

"What do we tell them?" asked Tobin.

The fox brushed some ash from her face. "To be watchful," she said. "Nothing more."

"Nothing more?" Bismark scoffed. "We must tell them to flee! To run from this bloodthirsty monster!"

"It may not be bloodthirsty. And it may not be a monster. And it is definitely not a dragon." Dawn held her head high, her voice steady. The fox gazed at the smoky, gray sky and gathered her breath. She didn't believe dragons were real, but nothing else seemed to explain the raining ash, the smoldering trees, and the huge gash in the earth. "We don't have enough information."

Tobin nodded in agreement, but his beady eyes remained fixed on Dawn. "How serious is this?" he asked, searching his friend's face for signs of comfort. All he could see, though, was the tense twitch of her jaw as she stared off into the clouds. The pangolin cradled his stomach, which twisted in terror.

"We don't know yet. And even if it is some sort of...large, predatory animal," Dawn said, cautiously glancing at Bismark, "it may have fled far from here."

Tobin took a deep breath. Though his throat was still scratchy with ash, the air was clearing. As the moon worked its way through the clouds, the land brightened, and the familiar shadows of night took their place. "Yes," agreed Tobin, "maybe it's gone."

"Wait—hold on *un momentito*—what is that?" Bismark's voice cracked as he pointed into the distance, his tiny paw shaking with fear. Desperately, he leaped toward the fox and clung to her dust-coated leg.

The fox spun around. A long, dark shadow stretched across the ground. It had four thick legs and a long tail. A row of sharp spikes ran the length of its spine.

The Brigade watched in silence as the shadow grew larger and larger as the figure moved closer and closer. It was heading directly their way.

25

Chapter Four
THE STRANGER

"Show yourself at once!" Bismark commanded. He tightened his grip on the fox's hind leg, only daring to peek out for a moment. "We are prepared to fight, no matter how long your fangs or how sharp your spikes!"

Terror filled Tobin's eyes. "We...we are?" A small poof escaped from his rear.

"*Mon dieu*!" Bismark exclaimed, plugging his nose with his paw. "Can't you at least aim the other way? Toward the ferocious fiend that approaches us?"

A sudden harsh wind swept through the air, sending a chill down the pangolin's spine and kicking up the soot at his feet. The wind continued to blow, and soon enough, the Brigade was cloaked in a thick, sandy spiral of dirt. Flying bits of stone, some as large as chestnuts, swirled all around them.

"I can't see!" Tobin cried as he curled himself into a ball.

"Well, I can't *breathe!*" Bismark coughed. "Your stench has completely surrounded me! And now a fleck of ash has flown into my big, beautiful peepers!" The sugar glider crouched and covered his eyes with his flaps.

But Dawn remained standing, determined to see through the dust. Determined to see the creature that headed toward them. She ducked, dodging a black rock that whistled overhead. The swirling ash played tricks on her eyes, making monsters appear and disappear out of the churning air. Reluctantly, the fox hunkered down and covered her face with her paws.

When the wind had at last eased, the Brigade remained huddled close. They could hear the sound of shuffling footsteps.

"Oh *mon dieu!*" With his flaps still shielding his face, Bismark prepared for the worst. "Is it close?" he sputtered. "I think I feel its breath on my neck! *Mon dieu*! *Mon dieu*! I hope it's not hungry!"

Dawn opened her eyes just a crack. "Look," she whispered.

Though the shadow had drawn closer, it looked smaller now.

What was the creature's true size? Dawn, Bismark, and Tobin wondered, holding their breath, waiting to see.

Finally, the figure stepped into a lone beam of moonlight. The Brigade-mates exhaled. It was no larger than Tobin.

"Ha! *That's* the puny thing you two were scared of? I knew this monster was all shadow, no substance!" The sugar glider gave a light-hearted wave of his flap and tossed his head back in triumph.

Dawn, however, stood steady as a stone and sank her claws into the ground. Tobin remained close to her side, though he had to admit, there seemed to be no reason for his fears of giant monsters. But as he glanced back at the crater, he could feel doubt gnawing at his gut—something must have caused it, after all. Something big.

"Come, ma chérie," beckoned Bismark. "Let us approach as a couple."

The fox took a single step forward and squinted

into the dust. The reptilian creature drew closer, its features growing clearer. It had greenish-gray skin, and the angular jaw of an iguana. Its long, spiked tail whipped behind it with every step.

Bismark spun and twirled, trying his best to make an impression. "Well, hello there, newcomer!" He raised his flap in an awkward salute. "Please, *por favor*—state your name and your purpose."

The creature paused just a flap's length away from the sugar glider, but it did not speak.

Bismark scanned the foreigner with his round, dark eyes. "Hmm," he mused, mischievously stroking his chin. "I have a feeling she's of the female persuasion, *amigos*. I'll handle this."

He cleared his throat. "*Buon giorno*, beautiful stranger." He lowered his high-pitched voice so it sounded as romantic as possible. Looking over his shoulder, making sure Dawn could see, he scrunched his nose and shook his head. This creature was no beauty.

With her glassy dark eyes and fearsome spikes, her appearance was stony and cruel—like an ancient being from an old, forgotten time. But as frightening as she appeared, it was difficult for Bismark to look away from her. Her features were remarkable: the orange dots around her thick neck, the neon-blue streaks lining her eyes, the eerie sheen of her skin. And most of all, the mysterious flicker of light, like a halo, that gleamed from the top of her head.

"Do not be so shy, my spiky sugar plum, my ravishing reptile."

The stranger still said nothing.

"Mmm, I see," murmured the sugar glider. "The strong and silent type. *Me gusta!*"

"Bismark," hissed Dawn. "Stand back." The fox shifted her weight. She had never seen a creature like this before. Warily, she eyed the row of spikes that ran from the newcomer's head to the tip of her tail. The longer, sharper prongs in the middle line of her back looked particularly wicked, though the shorter barbed bands on either side appeared menacing as well. The fox's breath caught in her throat.

Tobin looked at the creature, standing small and still in the ash. Though he trusted the fox, a twinge of sympathy stung his heart. Yes, the reptile was unfamiliar. But he had once been a stranger himself, timid, scared, and alone.

Carefully, he ventured toward this outsider and looked kindly into her eyes. They were gold with black slits for irises. "Can...can we help you?" he asked.

The reptile met Tobin's gaze and repeatedly

blinked, as though studying the presence before her. Finally, she opened her mouth and spoke. "No," she replied. Her tone was flat and low. "But I can help you." Slowly, she closed her eyes and bowed her head, revealing the top of her scale-covered skull. Then, without warning, the grayish-green surface burst open, exposing a gleaming, round orb. The creature had a third eye.

Chapter Five
THE THIRD EYE

Tobin froze in surprise. Though the creature also stood still, the moonlight flickered off the top of her head, making it seem as if she were moving. As the clouds above shifted the shadows, the pangolin grew aware of his silence.

Make her feel welcome, he thought. He was usually quite good at that. But when he opened his mouth to speak, no words came out. Unsure of what else to do, the pangolin stepped away from the creature, his jaw still hanging slack.

But while Tobin moved back toward the fox, Bismark bounded forward, mesmerized. The stranger remained still and calm.

Interpreting her silence as permission, the sugar glider eagerly stood on his toes, bent over the mysterious eye, and stared into its depths. It shone with a strange glow, as though lit from within. "*Mon dieu*! It's like a moonstone," he said, leaning closer, captivated by his milky reflection.

"Bismark," snapped Dawn. With a sharp flick of her head, the fox gestured for him to back up.

The reptile smirked. "Don't worry, fox," she said smoothly. "This reaction is not unusual."

The hair on Dawn's neck pricked on end. With her gaze still fixed on the reptile, she extended a paw toward the sugar glider and pulled him back by his flap.

"What?" Bismark squealed, innocently shrugging his shoulders. "You heard the...uh, reptile. My reaction was not unusual!"

"But *she* is," hissed Dawn.

The sugar glider shuddered at his friend's steely tone and eyed her tight grip on his flap. "Don't be jealous, *amore*," he chuckled. "She has nothing on you! Well, besides that extra eye, I suppose." The sugar glider paused and tilted his face up toward Dawn's. "But look at us!" he exclaimed. "*I* have two eyes, *you* have two eyes—we were made for each other!"

The fox released her hold on the sugar glider and took a bold step toward the stranger. "You said you could help us."

The reptile grinned, exposing three rows of teeth: two on top, one on bottom.

"Holy smokes!" Bismark gasped. His eyes ran the length of the creature. "Do you have three of *everything*?"

Eyeing the stranger's fangs, Dawn bared her own, each as sharp as a needle.

"Let's start over," offered the reptile. Though her voice sounded kind and polite, her eyes remained hard and cold. "My name is Polyphema and I am a tuatara."

"Tutu-what?" Bismark asked. "Tutu-who?"

The stranger released a warm laugh, exposing her teeth once again. Although she had many, there were gaps between them where some were missing. And a large number of those that remained appeared to be worn down to nubs. "A tuatara."

"I'm sorry," Tobin said bashfully, "but I've never heard of a tuatara."

"That's no surprise," said the reptile. Her smile quickly turned down at the sides. "There are nearly none of us left."

"Oh goodness," gasped Tobin. "That's awful."

35

"Yes, it is," replied Polyphema. "But I prefer not to dwell on all that." She lifted her chin toward the moon.

"Why are you here?" demanded the fox. She took another step forward, stirring a small cloud of ash. The wind picked up a little, throwing a stinging wave of tiny rocks over them all.

Tobin drew in a breath. There was an obvious edge to Dawn's voice, and it made his heart lurch in his chest. Why was she being so harsh?

He looked at his new acquaintance: nearly extinct, yet so strong. He smiled, admiring this strange tuatara. But then he saw his leader: determined, intense, and reliable. Suddenly, he was not sure what to think. Was he supposed to be taking sides?

"I told you, I am here to help," said Polyphema. "Do you see that?" she asked, pointing at the gigantic hole in the earth. "Do you see what's at the bottom of it?

The three Nocturnals turned back to face the crater. Tobin blinked. With the arrival of the strange, three-eyed creature before him, he had nearly forgotten about the large shape pressed into the earth below, the shape that had scared him so badly before.

"*Bien sûr!*" replied Bismark. "How could we miss it? Just because we have two eyes and not three does not make us blind."

"Well, what do you see?" asked Polyphema.

The sugar glider scratched at his bald spot. "Isn't it obvious, Tutu? I see the monstrous mark of a beast!"

"Yes," the tuatara agreed, "but I see something more." She paused, then dramatically closed all three eyes, as though searching for some sort of vision. "I see the beast itself."

"Oh goodness!" gasped Tobin. Quickly, he coiled into a ball. "Where?" His voice echoed from deep beneath his scales. "What do we do? Is it close?"

"No, no," Polyphema assured him. "It's not here."

The pangolin breathed a short sigh of relief and uncurled his body. Then he scrunched his long snout. "I don't understand, though," he murmured. "You said that you see it." He surveyed the land. His eyesight was poor so he never relied much on his eyes. And with the tuatara having one extra? He certainly trusted her vision over his own.

"Yes," said the tuatara, "I do." She paused, and the scales on her speckled neck twitched. "I see it. I have only to concentrate and it comes to me, as if in a dream. I see you. I see everyone. I see the past, the present, the future. I see all with the power of my third eye. And there?" She nodded toward the menacing mark in the crater. "I see destruction to come. I see death."

37

"Death?" gasped the pangolin. He drew his scales close to his body and fought the urge to curl into a ball again.

Polyphema leaned her head down low, revealing her third eye once more. "Yes, death."

"Oh *mon dieu*!" Bismark cried. He flailed his flaps, creating a whirlwind of ash. "We are doomed! Done! *Fini*!"

Tobin took a deep breath. Then, suddenly, as if drawn by an invisible force, he gazed into the tuatara's strange, milky orb. "What do you mean exactly?" he asked quietly. "Do you see this beast causing death?"

"Yes," said Polyphema. "And my power of sight never fails."

Dawn let out a skeptical grunt. She found Polyphema's so-called visions difficult to believe.

But Polyphema pressed on, unbothered by the fox's distrust. "Don't worry," she said to the pangolin. Her spikes gleamed under the stars as she spoke. "I see death, as I've said." Her mouth spread into a sly, toothy grin. "But I also see how to escape it. I can tell you how to fight the beast."

Chapter Six
EYE TO EYE

"Well, don't just stand there, my mysterious, Tutu. Tell us how to stop this terrible creature!"

Polyphema looked at the sugar glider and tilted her scaly neck. "It is really quite easy," she said. "To defeat him, simply meet his demand." She paused, flicking her two front eyes over her audience. Her voice was low and unwavering. "Everyone must leave," she said. "The jerboas in the forest, the moles underground, even the birds in the sky. They all must leave the valley and never return."

For a moment, no one spoke. Only the wind shrieked in the night.

"*What*?" Bismark extended his flaps in disbelief, sending a whirlwind of ash through the air. "Impossible! Unworkable! Infeasipracticable!"

"Kick everyone out of their homes?" Tobin asked. The pangolin rubbed his round belly, which had suddenly developed a knot. "Why would the beast want that?"

"This is his territory," said Polyphema. "He came here first, long ago. Now he's returned to take what is rightfully his."

Dawn narrowed her eyes. "We will not force anyone out because of the demands of a selfish beast."

"I don't see any other choice," said the tuatara.

Slowly, with purpose in her stride, Dawn moved toward Polyphema, spearing the ground with her nails. They stood face to face, eye to eye, with only a thin veil of ash hanging between them. "These animals are not going anywhere," said Dawn. Her words pierced the air like shards of ice.

"But look what the beast has already done!" exclaimed Polyphema. With a flick of her head, she gestured toward the burned ground and the ragged crater nearby.

Dawn shrugged. "There's no proof that the beast did this," she said.

The moonlight peeked through the clouds, flickering off Polyphema's scales. "Trust me. This is the work of an angry, powerful creature."

Tobin curled into a ball. With the exception of the wind's lonely howl, the air hung heavy with silence.

"Well then," said Dawn, clearing her throat. "I will go talk to the beast. We will hear for ourselves exactly what he is planning, and exactly what he wants."

Slowly, Tobin uncoiled. He stared at the fox in awe.

Bismark, however, let out a quick yelp. "*Muchacha*, no!" With a dramatic leap, he flung himself at the fox and clutched the red fur on her leg. "You can't! You won't! I won't let you!"

Polyphema's eyes flickered. "We have to remove everyone from the area!" she exclaimed, her voice ringing with desperation. "We need to do what he says! I have seen the future."

"We will trust what we see for ourselves," Dawn said coolly. With a confident turn of her head, she looked toward her friends. "Let's go."

The tuatara gazed down at the ground for a moment. "You have no idea what you're in for," she murmured, sweeping the ash with her tail. And then, with a narrowed stare, she watched the Brigade depart into the dust.

Chapter Seven
UP

As the trio left, Bismark turned for one last look at the reptile. With each step they took, she grew smaller and fainter, her scales fading into the ash. "Do not cry, darling Tutu!" he called over his tiny shoulder. "Though you will never meet another brigade like ours, nor another glider so handsome as myself, I am sure you and your magic eye shall survive well into the future!"

Tobin edged alongside the crater. Timidly, he glanced over its rim at the monstrous print down below.

His scales started to shudder. "I don't know, Bismark," he said. "It doesn't seem like she needs us. It seems like *we* might need *her*."

The sugar glider threw back his head and placed a paw on his chest. "My silly *amigo!*" he chortled. "Everyone needs me. But I agree—I think we do need that triple-eyed Tutu."

Dawn let out a grunt of annoyance.

"Don't be jealous, *princessa*. I need you as well. It's just—instead of your eyes, I desire your heart."

"I'm not jealous," she said. "I am wary." The fox surveyed the lifeless, gray landscape and the deep crater beside her. Her gaze hardened. "I admit that I do not know who or what this beast is. What I do know, however, is that the tuatara's 'solution' is no solution at all." She took a deep breath, calming her racing pulse. "In order to solve this problem, we must go to the source."

Tobin gulped. "B-b-but the source of this problem is the b-b-beast."

"Precisely," said Dawn. She turned her gaze toward the looming, black mountain ahead. "And our best chance of spotting him is from that peak."

"Oh goodness," groaned Tobin. The pangolin was not the best rock climber. Compared to his friends' legs, Tobin's legs were stumpy and stout, which often caused him to fall behind. Nevertheless, he followed Dawn's lead, past the crater, trudging through the vast field of ash until they reached the foot of the mountain. As he surveyed the steep slope, Tobin's chest tightened.

From afar, the mountain appeared dark and eerie, but its face, at least, had looked smooth. Up close though, its surface was rocky and jagged. Large boulders had splintered into razor-sharp shards that threatened to cut his paws.

Tentatively, the pangolin extended a foot and touched it to the dark stone.

"It's okay!" Dawn called out. The nimble fox was already several ledges above on the slope.

"*Si, si,* cautious comrade! Come along, now! It's really quite easy!" Bismark cheered.

Tobin squinted up at him. Bismark was perched comfortably on the arch of Dawn's back. The pangolin sighed and slowly, carefully, started to climb.

By the time he reached the halfway point, he was huffing and puffing. For as the height increased so, too, did the number of loose rocks sliding down from the top. And with every step he took, a thick, suffocating cloud rose around him. He was exhausted, and breathing in all this ash made his lungs feel weak.

"I don't know...if this...is such a good...idea,"

Tobin uttered between coughs. He stopped to catch his breath.

"Just a little farther," Dawn insisted.

Tobin wiped his watery eyes and inspected his tired paws. They were rubbed raw. "Just follow the white of Dawn's tail," he said to himself.

But this proved quite difficult. As Tobin climbed higher and higher, the wind grew stronger, whipping across his scales and stinging his face. Spirals of gray sand and dirt swirled through the air, blinding him. At times, his friends disappeared from view, completely lost in the shadowy wind, and the pangolin had to pause and wait for the flicker of Dawn's white tail to re-emerge.

Finally, the climbers stopped.

"Over here," called the fox. She was perched on a pointed ledge that stuck out over the slope.

"Oh, thank goodness," gasped Tobin. With a series of grunts, the pangolin clambered up the last stretch of stone and heaved himself up on the ledge, tumbling over its rim in a clumsy heap.

"See?" said the fox. "From this height, we have a good view."

"*Absolutamente*," agreed Bismark, batting his eyes at the fox.

Tobin peered over the edge and grew dizzy.

Quickly, he rose to all fours and scuttled as far back as possible. "I didn't realize we'd climbed so high," he gasped. The pangolin pressed his body against the stony gray wall of the mountain and attempted to steady his breath. His heart was pounding.

"Don't worry," Dawn said. The fox was fearlessly perched at the rim of the ledge, and she squinted toward the horizon. "Just keep your eyes peeled for anything unusual or for a sign of the beast."

But Tobin's chest remained tight. He had been concentrating so hard on walking up the steep mountain and keeping his balance that he had nearly forgotten why they were there. Yes, he had survived the treacherous climb, and he was beginning to feel steady on the ledge, but what was next? Would they spot this strange, evil creature? And what would happen if they did? A shiver ran down his spine. Perhaps the worst was yet to come.

Chapter Eight
THE FORTRESS

Mustering his last bit of courage, Tobin crept toward the fox, who still remained standing on the edge of the ledge. His paws trembled and his scales quivered. Images of a gigantic monster ripping its way through the land tore through his mind.

But when Tobin inched next to Dawn and squinted into the distance, he saw no such sight. In fact, except for the crater—which looked much smaller from here—there was nothing to see at all. There was no movement. No color. No life. With its thick coat of ash and sparse sprinkling of trees, the land looked still and gray. The area resembled a dark, forgotten graveyard. Even though it was a bleak view, Tobin exhaled a sigh of relief.

"Let's look on the other side," Dawn said. Moving carefully, she walked along the ledge, which circled the mountain. Bismark rode on her back, and Tobin followed, staying as far from the edge as possible.

"Bismark," Dawn said, "do you see anything here?"

"Just the bright bushy tail of my one true love." He swooned.

The fox glanced over her shoulder. Her brow furrowed with disapproval. "Other way, Bismark," she chided.

The sugar glider replied with an innocent shrug.

"Wait a moment," said Tobin, "I think I see something after all. There, on the ground." The pangolin craned his short, armored neck and rubbed his small, dark eyes.

Immediately, the fox spun back and followed her friend's gaze. "It looks like a mound of rocks," she said.

"Oh goodness." Tobin sighed. "That's not very unusual or helpful. I'm sorry."

Dawn narrowed her keen, amber eyes. Something appeared a bit strange. The rocks weren't exactly a mound—they were stacked upon one another, forming more of a tower. It was circular in shape—about the height of a tree, but wider. And though it looked hollow, the opening on top was partially blocked, as if someone had scattered sticks over it.

"What is it, my sweet?" asked Bismark. "What do your lovely, amber eyes behold?"

"I'm not sure," murmured Dawn. "It almost looks like ... a fortress."

"What?" The sugar glider squeezed between his two friends. "Let me see."

The Brigade-mates peered down.

"I don't know," Tobin said. A deep rumble rose from his belly. The pangolin was always hungry for a tasty snack, and it felt like ages since he had last eaten. "From this height, the rocks just look like beetles." He paused. "Or ants, dipped in a little bit of honey." He licked his lips as his thoughts turned completely to food. He closed his eyes. Visions of tender termites danced in his head.

Following his nose, Tobin wandered off to the side in search of a juicy morsel. *Those two don't need me now anyway,* he thought. *My eyesight is too poor to be of any real use. And I'll be much more alert when my tummy is full.* Tobin nodded, convincing himself. He climbed down onto a lower ledge and began to explore it. "I'll go back once I sniff out a tasty snack."

Then he stopped. His imaginary feast was interrupted by a strange noise from above—a crackling of sorts. It sounded like sparks shooting out of a fire. The pangolin cocked his head. The sound grew louder, heavier, closer, until it rang like thunder in his ears. He looked up. A dark wave of rocks was tumbling right toward him, crushing all that stood in its path. Tobin froze in fear.

"Tobin! Watch out!" Dawn's shrill cry jolted the paralyzed pangolin.

Frantically, he scrambled back toward his friends. He took a running jump and clawed his way up to where Dawn and Bismark were standing. Gasping and panting, Tobin turned his head to see the rockslide smash the spot where he'd stood just moments before.

"Are you all right?" asked the fox. She bent over her friend with concern.

"Are you kidding?" cried Bismark. "He's more than all right… he's *magnifico*!" The sugar glider gave Tobin a firm pat on the back. "We should give you a nickname to honor your newfound speed. Perhaps speedy-scales, crazy-claws, zippety-zoo!"

"Oh goodness," gasped Tobin, finally recovering his breath. "That rockslide came out of nowhere!"

Dawn narrowed her eyes and stood tall. "Yes," she murmured. Her voice was tinged with suspicion. "It certainly did."

Chapter Nine
THE SUSPECT

"By all that glides!" shouted Bismark, pacing back and forth. "It was the beast! We have experienced his rage firsthand!"

Tobin's eyes widened. "Oh goodness!" he cried. "Have we angered it by coming up here?"

"I have no doubt he wants us gone, *amigo*! Word in the woods is that this beast fellow gets territorial!"

"Bismark," said Dawn, "what are you talking about? There is no 'word.'"

"Potato, potahto. Pomelo, pomahlo." Bismark waved his paw. "Point is, that's one bad beast. Our friend Polywollydingdong was right."

"Polyphema," said Dawn with a sigh.

"Yes, right, that's what I said."

Dawn held up her paw to shush Bismark. "We still haven't seen the beast. Don't you think that's a little odd if he's a giant?"

Bismark scratched his bald spot. "Do you need to see the air to know it's there, *mon amour*? Do you need to see my love to know it exists?"

Dawn paced toward the rim of the ledge and narrowed her almond-shaped eyes. She surveyed the expanse of dark dust below. Then she gazed at the jagged rocks perched above. "No," she began, "but—"

"But *nada*, my darling! I know you and Tutu aren't the bestest of friends, but I see no evidence to prove her wrong!" Bismark stood tall and punched a small fist in the air. "I object to your objection!"

Dawn looked again at the barren, gray landscape then thoughtfully scanned the horizon. "What if it was her?" she asked suddenly. "What if Polyphema caused the rockslide herself?"

Tobin glanced at his leader. "I… I was sure it was the beast," he stammered. "Those rocks came so fast."

"It was definitely the beast!" Bismark insisted. He clicked his tongue at Dawn. "Why are you so anti-Tutu? Hmm?" Bismark patted Dawn's paw. "I hate to say it, my love, but your jealousy has clouded your judgment. That reptile Poly... Poly..."

"Polyphema?" said Tobin.

"Yes, *si*, whatever." Bismark cleared his throat. "Our new friend's third eye is quite a remarkable feature, and I'm sure she has *mucho* talent for seeing the future, but the rocks? *Impossible*! How would she have arrived here in time?" The sugar glider shook his small head. "No, no, no. Her legs are far too stumpy to move that fast. In fact, they're not so unlike those of our favorite pangolin." Bismark tilted his head toward Tobin.

Dawn shrugged her shoulders.

"Come!" The sugar glider spun on his heel. "We must track down the culprit! I'll tackle him myself if I have to!" Bismark flexed his scrawny biceps then led them back around the mountain so that they looked out over the crater. Nearing the edge, he eyed the monstrous print at the bottom of the enormous hole. Though it seemed quite small from this height, he remembered how large it was up close. He gulped. "I shall still be victorious," he murmured. "Size and strength are no match for pure genius!"

Tobin turned to face Dawn. Her expression remained skeptical. "Bismark has a point," he said meekly. "You know, not about his genius, but about the beast. And Polyphema *did* warn us."

Dawn looked to her friend and considered his words.

"That rockslide scared me," Tobin continued, his beady eyes wide with fright. "I'm not as brave as you are. I'm afraid of the beast."

The fox nodded. The rockslide could have been the work of the beast. It was possible. "You're right," Dawn said softly.

Tobin's expression turned hopeful. "So we'll go back to Polyphema and talk to her?"

Dawn gazed at the blurry horizon. Then she noticed a small figure near the edge of the crater. It was Polyphema, who seemed to be waiting for them. "Yes," she replied. Her taut muscles slightly relaxed. "The tuatara may be right after all."

Chapter Ten
A CLEVER PLAN

"We're baaaa-aaaaack!" With a somersault and a leap, Bismark barreled back toward the crater where Polyphema still stood. "Did you miss me, dear Tutu? Yes, *oui*, of course you did—how could you not?"

"I thought you might be back soon," she replied. Her lips curled in a slight grin. "I believe you need my assistance?"

"Oh goodness, yes," replied Tobin. He trudged up behind Bismark and glanced over his shoulder. "I'm afraid we've angered the beast."

"Are you all right?" asked Polyphema, taking a step toward the pangolin.

Bismark quickly hopped between them, flaps outspread. "What about *moi*? I know I appear strong—almighty, some might say—but even the magnificent sugar glider is not invincible."

The tuatara cocked her head. "I don't see any injuries."

"Well, I *could* have been injured," Bismark muttered, turning away.

"And how are you, Tobin?" Polyphema looked the pangolin up and down. "Were you struck by the rocks?"

"Wait a moment," said Dawn. "We never mentioned the rocks." The fox stepped in front of Tobin protectively. "I was right," she snarled. "You know what happened. You were there!"

"Yes, of course, I know what happened," replied Polyphema. "But I wasn't there." The tuatara lowered her face, exposing the top of her head. "Have you forgotten, fox? I see all." The scales on her scalp parted, revealing her milky third eye.

Dawn's triumphant expression grew dim, but she still growled below her breath.

Bismark scurried between the two females,

placing a paw against each. "Let's focus on slaying the beast, not each other, *oui*?"

"I already told you," said Polyphema. "The beast won't strike if we clear the area. You have no other choice. He is too big to slay. Too smart to trap."

"And *I* already told *you*," replied Dawn, "that that will never happen. We will not banish our friends."

"Trap," murmured Bismark. The sugar glider, who still had a paw on each female, suddenly threw up his flaps. "Tutu, that's it!" he cried. "We can trap the beast. And I know just how to do it. It is genius, foolproof, *magnifico*!"

"Trap it?" Tobin said with a tremble.

"That sounds dangerous," said the fox. "I don't know if it's such a good idea."

"But *I* do! *I* know!" Bismark insisted. The sugar glider's face lit up. "Listen, my friends. *Écoutez*. First, we collect all the vines we can find. Then we weave them together so they hold nice and tight. Like so." The sugar glider hugged the fox to show what he meant before she quickly shook him off.

"Right," he continued, dusting his coat. "As I was saying, we weave the vines until we have a giant net, then we cast it over a hole. In this case," he gestured behind him, "that crater."

Tobin cocked his head. "Then what?"

"Then comes the fun part," said Bismark, his eyes flickering with mischief. "You see, the net will *look* natural. Once we cover it with ash, that is. So all we have to do is lure the beast onto it." Bismark shot a wink at his audience. "And then: *Boom! Bam! Splat!* The beast falls into the giant hole in the earth and we have him!" The sugar glider struck a triumphant pose, legs wide, paws on hips.

Dawn walked toward the deep, ragged crater and studied the size of it. "I don't know," she muttered. "It doesn't seem practical. In order to cover this hole and make sure that the beast stays trapped, our net would need to be enormous. We would need a huge number of vines, and it would take lots of hard work."

"*No problemo*," replied Bismark, casually waving a flap. He coughed at the dust it stirred up. "There are plenty of vines around here."

The Brigade eyed the landscape, gray and barren. Dotted here and there were the taller piles of ash that marked what was left of the plants.

"Well…there's some over there, at least." He gestured toward a far-off cluster of trees and shrubs with long, trailing stems. "And as for the work?" Bismark extended his paws before him, rubbed them against one another, and fixed his gaze on the fox. "'T'is nothing for these skillful paws. Strong, nimble, quick—yet gentle as well, I might add."

"I don't know," Dawn repeated.

Polyphema stepped to her side and nodded. "I agree. The plan will simply not work." The tuatara extended her neck so its creases stretched flat. Her scales shone in the moonlight. "Don't get me wrong, Bismark—it's clever, really. But the beast will not be so easily lured to his doom."

"Bah! And how would you know?"

Polyphema crept to the edge of the crater. "I know the beast well...." She paused. "I know how he thinks." The tuatara narrowed her eyes at the deep hole in the earth and the shape of the beast below. "He won't trust any bait you set for him, believe me."

With a deep bow, Bismark offered the tuatara his paw. "Then you must be a part of our scheme, Tutu-tata. Since you know him so well, you can be the one to draw the beast into the trap! He will trust you, no?"

Polyphema's tail flicked behind her. Her jaw was clenched.

"What is it, *amiga*? Are you worried about luring the beast?" The sugar glider threw an arm over the tuatara's back. "Oof!" Feeling the poke of her spikes, he recoiled in pain. "Do not worry, Poly-pee...Poly-poo…Poly…who?" Bismark scratched at his bald spot then started again. "Do not worry, Tutu. If you need any lessons on how to charm and command, you can ask me—the *maestro* himself!"

Polyphema stood still, lost in thought. Though her third eye remained shut, the scales on her head seemed to pulse, as if, even while hidden, the pale, white orb was at work. "Very well," she whispered at last. Amidst the moans of the wind, her voice sounded hollow and low. "I have seen a future where this plan succeeds."

"Woo-hoo!" yodeled Bismark. "This is the stuff of legends, *amigos.* For ages to come, animals will tell the tale of the brave Brigade's brilliant victory over the big, brutal beast of the night! That is, if we have our lovely leader's approval." He looked sideways at Dawn.

The fox took a deep breath. She knew that they might be facing great danger, and every moment they wasted in discussing this was a moment they could be doing something to stop the beast. It was already midnight, and at least Bismark had a plan.

Dawn nodded her head. "Let's do it," she said. "It's our only hope."

Bismark's bulbous eyes gleamed with excitement. "It's decided then!" he exclaimed, hopping atop a small rock. With his chin toward the sky and his cape shining bright, he punched his small fist in the air. "The Nocturnal Brigade traps the beast!"

Chapter Eleven
BEYOND THE WALL

"This net is going to be huge!" yelped Bismark. "Massive! Giant! Humongous!" Bismark was excited. But, suddenly, his eagerness turned into panic when he realized the enormous job that they faced. "*Ay, ay, ay!* We need help!" he cried, and he toppled off of his rock.

"Yes," said the fox. "Let's gather the animals of the valley. We need as many workers and as many vines as possible."

"Get help?" Polyphema tightened her claws. "I

told you—the beast wants the area clear! You can't bring more animals here! It's too dangerous. We must do this ourselves."

"Well, *si*, I could do all the heavy lifting myself, of course." Bismark puffed out his chest and flexed both his arms.

"I don't understand," murmured Dawn. "If this beast is as dangerous as you say…"

"…then we need to move fast!" finished Tobin.

The tuatara's eyes flashed with fear. "But—"

"My *amigos* are right," Bismark said, cutting off Polyphema. "We need as many helpers as possible. Plus—" Bismark mischievously stroked his chin, "—I do enjoy bossing around those jerboas…."

"The jerboas? Those little brown rodents?" Polyphema paused, lost in thought. Then, with a glance at the mountain, she nodded. "Well, I suppose they'd be fine…."

Dawn furrowed her brow, confused by the reptile's sudden change of heart. But there was no time to question things—they had to move quickly. "Bismark, Tobin, you must leave now. Bring help as fast as you can."

Tobin glanced at the fox. "Wait a moment," he started, his brow creased with concern. "What about you? Aren't you coming with us?"

"No," replied Dawn. "I will stay here and instruct the animals as they arrive."

The fox smiled sincerely at Tobin, then slyly at Polyphema. "Besides, with this giant beast on the loose, no one should be alone."

"Come along, comrade!" cried Bismark, giving Tobin a pat on the back. "With my brain, my brawn, and your, well, sturdy scales, we have nothing to fear—*nada*! Though it does pain me to leave these loveliest of lovelies, I must admit." He gazed at Polyphema and Dawn and let out a sigh.

"Come on, Bismark," urged Tobin, nudging his friend with his snout.

"Right, right. Off we go." As he trudged away, Bismark glanced longingly over his shoulder. "Toodle-loo, Tutu! Au revoir, Dawn, *mon amour*! Fare thee well, my sweet *bellas*!"

As Bismark and Tobin's shadows disappeared in the distance, Dawn and Polyphema stood in tense silence. They squinted at each other, neither blinking despite the wind and the ash that swirled around them.

"I'm going to go get some rest," said Polyphema. "It's been quite the evening."

Dawn gazed up. The sky was stained black and

the moon hung at its peak. "Aren't you a nocturnal?" she asked, puzzled.

The tuatara nodded. "Yes." Her voice slightly cracked. "I've just…well…I've been quite tired."

"Better get some rest, then," said Dawn.

Was Polyphema lying? Something about her excuse seemed false, but the fox did not let her doubt show. "I'll be collecting things we might need for the net," she said smoothly.

The animals spun on their heels and walked in opposite directions through the scorched plants and trees.

But not for long. Glancing over her shoulder, the fox waited for Polyphema's form to fade. Then, she switched her course and stalked the strange tuatara through the darkness.

Careful to keep plenty of distance between them, Dawn followed the reptile's tracks, tracing the snaking line of her tail in the ash. Soon enough, she found herself at the edge of the mountain. The fox slowed to a crawl. The rocky peak blocked the moon, and the night felt heavy and dark.

Dawn circled the mountain until she reached its opposite side. Then, suddenly, she stopped. Polyphema's tracks had led her to a wall made of large rocks. It was the strange structure they'd seen earlier from the mountaintop! The fox looked every which way, hoping to spot the reptile, or at least to pick up her tail line in the ash. But she was nowhere in sight, and the track ended here. Dawn furrowed her brow—there was only one possibility.

Crouching low in the shadows, the fox lifted her head to gaze up.

There she was—Polyphema—climbing the fortress's wall. The tuatara moved quickly and confidently, gripping the rocks with her claws, ascending the slope with ease. Step after step, stone after stone, she climbed higher, until finally she reached the top. For a moment, she paused. Her scales flickered under the moon and she drew in a breath. Then, in a quick flash of silver, she ducked into the tower, her tail vanishing below the stone rim.

Dawn stepped out from the shadows. What was the tuatara doing here? What was inside that stone fort?

She raised a paw to the rock, ready to make the climb, but then her paw slipped on the shaky surface, and the stone tumbled down to the ground. Dawn froze. She could hear rustling inside the fortress. Had Polyphema heard her outside? Nervously, the fox waited for any sign she'd been caught. But after several moments of silence, she relaxed and took a small step back.

Perplexed, Dawn gazed at the stone wall. She was nimble—able to climb almost anything. But this fortress was steep and unstable. How did the tired, old tuatara scale the wall with such ease? It didn't make sense... unless the trek was routine—something Polyphema did all the time.

The fox circled the structure. There had to be some sort of entrance—an opening that she could squeeze through—but the stones were stacked tightly with little to no room between. She sighed, discouraged. But then she heard something—a mumbling of sorts. Her heart leaped in her chest.

Dawn pressed an ear to the wall. There it was again! Mumbling... a voice...

Polyphema wasn't alone.

The tuatara was definitely speaking to someone. But who?

Chapter Twelve
SKREEEEEEEK!

Dawn listened closely. She pressed her ear tighter to the wall and tried to make out the words. Then...

SKREEEEEEEK!

A shrill squawk rang out through the night. Immediately, the mumbling inside the fortress stopped. For a moment, there was pure quiet. Then, there was a frantic rustle—a scramble, the sound of claws against stone. Polyphema was leaving the fortress... and fast!

Dawn's heart started to race. *I can't let her know*

that I followed her, she thought. *I can't let her see me!* The fox drew in a deep breath. Then, as fast as she could, she sprinted the way she came, around the base of the mountain and away from the mysterious fortress.

Dawn pushed herself to the limit, dashing across the ash-covered ground at breakneck speed, kicking up huge clouds of dust as she ran.

When she reached the crater nobody was there. She glanced behind her. No sign of Polyphema. Good. She had escaped unseen. For a moment, the fox sat and caught her breath. Then, from the shadows, she heard the snap of a twig.

She drew in a worried breath.

"Helloooooooo, *amiga*!"

With a grin on his face and his flaps outspread, Bismark appeared, twirling and hopping his way toward Dawn. Behind him, Tobin sputtered and coughed, struggling to keep up with his friend.

"Come on, *mon ami*! Chop-chop!"

Dawn took a step toward Bismark. "Where are the others?" she asked. "Did you bring help?"

"Y-yes," Tobin gasped, placing a claw on his heaving gut. "They're…coming. Just…a little…behind."

"I sprinted the whole journey back!" Bismark announced proudly. "I could not stand another moment away from my love, or from our new three-eyed friend." He batted his eyes. "Did you two have fun while we were away? Where is that lovely Tutu, anyway?"

"I'm here," said a low, raspy voice. The tuatara stepped out of the darkness into the moonlight. She was panting. Nervously, she looked up at the sky. "I was trying to sleep," she lied, "but then I heard a strange noise. It... it sounded like a bird!"

"That is the sound of help, *amiga!*" Bismark spun toward the shadows. "Hurry, slowpokes! *Vámanos!* Pick up the pace!"

The animals Bismark and Tobin had gathered from the valley approached the crater, shrouded in a large cloud of dust.

Polyphema craned her scaled neck toward the group. Her tail nervously twitched in the ash.

Dawn, with her keen amber eyes, looked out at the crowd. "Everyone's carrying vines," she observed. "Good work. Although the fox shifted her gaze toward Bismark's empty paws—"now I see why you got here first."

The sugar glider crossed his arms over his chest. "*Excusez-moi, muchacha,* but these flaps were preoccupied by tasks far more important than vine transport. You see, I, Bismark, *maestro extraordinaire* as

75

you might recall, was busy leading the way."

Tobin sighed and shook his long snout. Dawn raised a tawny brow.

"Please, *bella* Dawn," he continued. "I know you like looking at me, but perhaps you should direct your attention to all the other empty-pawed folk. Our scaly *amigo*, for instance? And the birdies?"

"I knew it!" cried Polyphema. "I knew I heard birds!" She glared at Bismark and Tobin. "You said you were only bringing jerboas!"

"Why should it matter?" said Dawn, narrowing her eyes. "We should be grateful to everyone here and make sure that they all feel welcome."

Polyphema shook her head. "The beast won't like this one bit," she said. Her third eye shot open and twitched with every beat of her heart. "No, he won't like this at all."

"Oh goodness," cried Tobin. "We're sorry! We didn't mean to do anything wrong!" The pangolin's body slumped with guilt, and he took a worried step back.

Bismark, however, leaped forward and stroked Polyphema's creased cheek. "Calm down, Poly-poo! The more, the merrier. These animals are here to help!" The sugar glider gestured toward the crowd. They had finally arrived, wheezing and sweating. "And look,"

Bismark continued, "I've got them totally under my flaps. *Regardez*." The sugar glider cleared his throat. "You may leave your vines here!" he shouted, extending his flaps with a flourish. The animals dropped their cargo to the ground. Bismark beamed at the crowd's obedience. Then he looked to his friends for approval. "You see that, Tutu? That's what we call respect."

But Polyphema paid no attention to the sugar glider's antics. She was distracted, rapidly blinking her eyes and frantically searching their surroundings. "Where are they?" she cried. "Where are the birds!?"

"Why all the attention on our winged friends, dear Tutu? Are you attracted to creatures who fly, like myself?" Bismark lifted his flaps and strutted proudly.

"Yes…" began Dawn, ignoring him. "What's going on here? Why so much interest in birds?"

"Just show me where they are," hissed the reptile. "I need to know… for the beast!"

Bismark sighed in exasperation. "Well, there are some right there, Poly-poo!" He gestured with a flap toward a group of round, ungainly birds, bumbling at the rear of the pack. "*Mon dieu*! For a creature with a whole extra peeper, you sure don't see much."

Polyphema followed the line of his paw toward a huddle of brown birds, short and squat with long beaks.

77

Clumsily, they teetered through the ash, poking around for roasted worms, often stepping on each other's feet. "You mean those things?" she asked in disbelief. "They don't even have wings."

"*Oui*, yes, it is a terrible truth." The sugar glider sighed. "The kiwis don't have wings. What can I say? Not all creatures are blessed with extraordinary features like mine."

Polyphema's lips curled in a grin, and a sound—almost like laughter—escaped from the edge of her mouth.

The fox cleared her throat. "What's so amusing?"

Quickly, the tuatara erased the grin from her lips. "N-nothing," she stammered. With serious eyes, she gazed at the fox. "You're right. We should make everyone here feel welcome."

Dawn studied Polyphema. She couldn't figure her out. But she would have to worry about that later.

The fox took a deep breath and climbed atop the large heap of vines. From that height, she could see everyone who had come to help. At the front, the jerboas squeaked and nervously scratched at their ears. Behind them, the kiwis whispered and wobbled in the thick layer of dust.

Dawn opened her mouth, prepared to speak to

SKREEEEEEEK!

the crowd. But then, before she could begin, a gust of wind hit her face and a dark, looming shadow swept over the ground.

SKREEEEEEEK!

Chapter Thirteen
A TERRIBLE WARNING

SKREEEEEEK!

The shrill sound came from above.

Everyone gazed up to see birds of prey soaring through the sky in a perfect V. A dramatic whoosh filled the night as hawks, falcons, and owls flapped their long wings in unison. Their sharp cries echoed through the dark. There were so many of them, their feathered silhouettes hid the moon.

"No!" A terrified scream pierced the air.

At once, the animals gasped and focused their eyes on its source—Polyphema.

For a moment, she froze, as though startled by her own cry. Then she bowed her head in embarrassment. "Excuse me," she said, her voice low. "I'm sorry. I... I...." Suddenly, she perked up. "I had a vision!" she said. The tuatara bowed to reveal her third eye. "An image of the past. Of terrible battles from long ago between the birds and the beast. And then a vision of things to come. Blood... feathers... broken beaks!" Her milky orb gleamed.

"Oh goodness!" shrieked Tobin.

"The birds do not stand a chance," warned Polyphema. "They must leave. The visions are growing more urgent. And they are never wrong."

"We've been over this," said Dawn, glaring at Polyphema. "No one is going anywhere."

The two females stared at each other. Finally, Polyphema's third eye twitched. She broke the fox's gaze. "You will regret this," she hissed. "And so will the birds." With a huff, the tuatara stepped away from the crowd.

Dawn narrowed her eyes at the reptile then quickly refocused. She had to remain calm and in control.

It was her job to manage the others.

She looked down at the helpers, who had grown in number. The birds of prey gathered around them, framing the smaller creatures in a band of bronze, gray, and pure white. The hawks scratched at the earth with their talons. The falcons darted their yellow-rimmed eyes. The owls swiveled their heads in quick circles. Feathers bristled and rippled like waves as the birds discussed the tuatara's warning.

Dawn stared at the many eyes looking up at her—orange and gold, big and small, oblong and round. They all shone with wonder and worry, and they were all fixed on her gaze. She felt a sudden swell in her chest. Then, the fox cleared her throat.

At once, the stirring ceased, and a hush fell over the crowd.

"Welcome," she said. "Thank you for coming. As you may know, there's—"

"A monster!"

"A terror!"

"A beast!"

The crowd erupted, buzzing and flapping with fear. The ash fluttered and swirled in the chaos.

"I told you not to alarm them!" Dawn said, shooting Bismark a glare.

The sugar glider's face burned a deep pink below his fur. "It—it was Tobin!"

The innocent pangolin raised his scaly brows in alarm.

Dawn rolled her eyes at Bismark, gave Tobin a knowing nod, and turned back to the crowd. "Yes," she said as calmly and evenly as she could. "There is a strange creature afoot. And it is responsible for the destruction you see."

The animals gasped as Dawn, the voice of reason and truth, confirmed what the dramatic, slightly less trustworthy sugar glider had told them earlier in the night.

"The children!" A kiwi's shrill voice rang from the rear of the crowd. "How will we save the children?" The distraught bird buried her beak in her husband's soft, hair-like feathers.

"Everyone, listen. There's no need to panic." Dawn's voice grew stronger and louder. "We will triumph over this beast. That's why you're here—to make a trap so we can catch it."

The hawks nodded their speckled heads. The owls hooted in agreement..

"Let's begin right away," Dawn continued. "The plan is to take the vines and make a net so that we can fool the beast into falling into the crater. Jerboas, remain here and begin weaving these vines together. Kiwis, travel to that far-off cluster and untangle those vines with your beaks. Owls, falcons, hawks—gather the vines from the kiwis and fly them back here." The fox paused and straightened her spine. "Does everyone know what to do?"

Despite their worry and the hard work that they faced, the crowd cheered.

"Woo-hoo!" Bismark yelped. "This calls for the flaps!" The sugar glider extended his wing-like flaps and prepared for a celebratory flight. But without the help of the wind, he barely rose off the ground before tumbling down in a heap. "Ahem...." Bismark scrambled to his feet and hastily dusted his coat, hoping that no one had seen. "Right..." he stammered. "like I was saying...let's trap this monster!"

Chapter Fourteen
ON THE HUNT

The fox descended from the mound of vines, and the animals began the hard work of making the net.

"Perfecto," sang Bismark. "Now that the workers are busy, only we, the elite, the special few, remain. Time to observe, instruct, and be glorious! Come, amigos. Tobin, Dawn, Poly-poo…" The sugar glider extended his flaps to beckon his friends. Then he scrunched his small face in confusion. "*Uno momento…* where's Tutu?"

Dawn scanned the surrounding landscape. It was buzzing with animals already at work, but Polyphema was nowhere in sight. "Strange," the fox murmured. "She was just here a moment ago. Very strange." She narrowed her amber eyes and searched the ground for the tuatara's tail markings. But she could detect not a single trace. "Well," said Dawn, "as long as we're alone... there's something I need to share with you." The fox paused, making sure no one lingered nearby. Then she leaned close to her friends. "Something odd happened while you were gone. Follow me."

Dawn led her friends toward the mountain.

Bismark eagerly bounded after the fox. "Where are you taking us, *ma chérie*? Have you found the beast? A pomelo tree? A romantic hideaway?" The sugar glider's face brightened, and he trailed the fox even closer so the fur on her tail swept his face.

As they walked farther around the mountain, Tobin realized how tired he was. "Oh goodness, it is getting late, isn't it?" He gazed at the sun, peeking over the horizon, and yawned. There had been so much traveling and alarm in the course of a single moon, and now it was past his bedtime.

"Just a little farther," urged Dawn, sensing her friend's exhaustion. She, too, was tired and her legs ached, but she needed to take her friends to the fortress. They had to find out who Polyphema had been talking to. Dawn quickened her pace, despite the pain in her limbs.

At last, with heavy breath, the Brigade arrived at the stone tower. In the early light of the morning, its rocks shone a pale orange.

"It's the fortress we saw from the mountain," said Tobin. "Why did you bring us here?"

Dawn motioned for the group to stay quiet. "Earlier, when I followed Polyphema, she climbed inside," she whispered. "Do you see her?" The fox's tawny fur stood on end, and her eyes scanned the tower for signs of movement. Was the tuatara here? Was she hiding nearby?

Bismark looked left and right. "Nope! *Nada.* Sorry, my love. No three-eyed Tutu."

Dawn nodded slowly. "Good," she said. The fur on her back relaxed. "That means we can search."

Tobin furrowed his brow. "Search for what?"

"For whomever Polyphema was talking to." The fox tilted her snout toward the fortress. "I heard mumbling. She was speaking to someone inside."

Tobin's eyes widened. "Oh goodness! Do you think…" he gulped, "do you think it was the beast?"

89

"What? *Nonsensimo!*" exclaimed Bismark. "The big bad beast? Cooped up in there? No, no, no." He nervously laughed and backed up.

But the fox moved forward. "We need to get closer," she whispered.

"Whoa there, *muchacha!* Have you lost your mind?" The sugar glider threw up his flaps. "Enough of this detective work. Listen to your trusty Bismark and come back with me. I have animals to command at the crater!"

Ignoring her friend, Dawn pressed her ear to the stone. Hesitantly, Tobin followed, making sure to keep his scales quiet against the rock. Finally, Bismark joined with a sigh.

Moments passed. The trio closed their eyes, straining to hear any sound. Anything to indicate a creature lurking on the other side of the wall. But there was nothing—just the low, cold hum of the wind.

Dawn took a seat on the ground and let out a grunt of frustration.

Bismark, though, chuckled, relieved. "Don't be disappointed, *ma chérie.* Be grateful, be thrilled! Don't you know what this means? Polyphema is innocent. She was talking to no one. Now *vamanos!* Let's go." The sugar glider shuffled away. "The beast is off doing beast things. No need for us to stay here and wait for his deadly return."

But still, Dawn hesitated and lingered next to the fortress.

"Really, Dawn, there seems to be nothing here," said the pangolin. "Let's go back to the crater and help build the net."

"*Si*. It's been a long night, and you have breathed in *mucho* ash. Perhaps it has gone to your head and you imagined that strange mumbling sound!"

"No, I didn't," Dawn argued. "There's someone in there." Her eyes shone with determination. "I'll prove it to you."

The fox placed her paw on a stone, attempting to climb the wall once again. But, just as it did before, the tower started to shake as soon as she gave it her weight.

"What are you doing, *princessa*?" cried Bismark. "Are you out of your beautiful mind?"

Dawn took another step up.

"Come down!" Tobin cried. "You'll get hurt!" The worried pangolin covered his eyes with his claws, recalling his close call with the rockslide just hours ago.

"I need to see what's inside," said the fox.

"We need you," stressed the pangolin.

Dawn looked up at the top of the fortress, then

below at her two Brigade-mates. Finally, with a sigh, she climbed back down.

"*Mon dieu!*" Bismark cried. "This jealousy you have for Tutu is really making you *loco*! Now listen," he said, cuddling up to the fox, "we've been over this. Polyphema is no threat at all! Yes…she has a third eye, and her spikes are strangely attractive, but you know you're my *numero uno*!" He embraced the fox's front leg. "These 'mumblings' you heard must have been your own thoughts of true love for me!"

Dawn gazed at the fort, the pangolin, then the sugar glider. "This is not a joke," she stressed. "I heard real voices. They were not thoughts of you." Frustrated, she flung Bismark off of her paw. "Someone's here… and whoever it is could be dangerous!"

Bismark raised his flaps to his face in shock. He knew that sometimes his silly remarks annoyed the more serious fox, but she had never responded like this. "W-well then," he stammered, "perhaps I should go where I'm wanted."

"Bismark, that's not what I meant—" Dawn said hurriedly. The Brigade always worked together. It was important they remained united and that Bismark stayed by her side.

But the sugar glider cut off the fox. "If anyone

needs me, I will be back at the crater," he announced, "where animals adore and respect me! *Adios*!"

And with that, Bismark spun on his heels and marched away through the ash.

Chapter Fifteen
OTTO

"Oh goodness," sighed Tobin, "I hope Bismark's all right." The pangolin squinted into the distance, hoping to catch sight of his friend.

"We'll find him later, and I will apologize. But I want to give this place one last look," said the fox.

Tobin nodded halfheartedly.

Dawn paused for a moment and placed a friendly paw on her friend's scaly back. "Trust me," she said. "We—"

Whoosh!

Whee!

Zoom!

Tobin's heart leaped in his chest. Something above them—he could not be sure what—was whipping and whirling through the pale morning sky. "Oh goodness!" he cried. He squinted in the unfamilar daylight. "What is that?"

Dawn's amber eyes darted as she tracked the airborne, zigzagging object. It was flying too fast and too wildly to tell what it was. As soon as she had it in her sight, it had banked off in a completely unpredictable direction. And now it was headed straight toward her! "Look out!" she cried, ducking low to the ground.

Tobin followed, dropping the smooth skin of his belly to the ash-covered earth. He felt a swoosh of air over his scales, then watched with horror as the flying thing catapulted past him and crashed straight into the stump of an elm tree.

"Oof!"

The fox and the pangolin shared a look of bewilderment. Then they headed to the tree stump. Poking up from the trunk's oval hollow, was a brown, feathered rear end.

"Are you okay?" Tobin asked, cautiously stepping forward.

96

"Oh! Oh golly gee!" The bird twitched back and forth in a frenzy as he attempted to unplug his head from the tree stump. After a few, unfruitful attempts, he gave up, allowing his tail feathers to slump and fall slack. "Well," he sighed, "I'm afraid I'm stuck. Stuck in a stump. Typical Otto. Typical, typical Otto." The bird kicked at the bark in frustration and let out a disgruntled huff that echoed through the log.

"Don't worry," said the pangolin. "We'll help you out of there."

Dawn nodded then carefully grabbed the bird's midsection. Tobin took hold on the opposite side, and the animals counted:

"One... two..."

On "three," they pulled, and the bird sprang from the log with a *pop*, sending the three animals tumbling back in a heap.

Quickly, the bird flapped to his feet, dusting himself free of ash and plucking small bits of bark from his feathers. "How embarrassing," he muttered. "How absolutely mortifying."

Tobin boosted himself to his feet and prepared to comfort the bird. He was usually quite skilled at putting others at ease. But when he rubbed the soot from his eyes and took in the newcomer, he could not help but recoil in shock.

For the most part, Otto was a traditionally handsome owl. His deep, brown feathers were dotted with pure white spots, as though sprinkled with large flakes of snow, and his eyes were striking and round. Even in the bleached morning light, they shone a bright, piercing gold. The problem was his neck.

Tobin gathered his paws at his chest. He knew, of course, that owls could rotate their heads. But Otto's head was tilted unnaturally, permanently cocked toward his shoulder. The pangolin gulped. It looked so strange and unstable that Tobin feared it might topple off.

"Oh…oh goodness," fumbled the pangolin. He turned to Dawn, hoping she would know how to react. But even the usually unruffled fox was perturbed.

"Oh golly, what is it?" asked Otto. "Is my beak scratched up? Are my feathers all out of sorts?"

Tobin shook his snout back and forth. "Nothing like that," he began. "It's just, well, when you crashed into that tree, or perhaps when we tugged you out…" The pangolin tilted his neck to the side to illustrate the rest of his thought.

At this, the owl exhaled, and a wave of relief swept his face. "Ohhhhh, my *neck*! Yes, of course."

Dawn and Tobin stared back at him blankly.

"Don't worry about *that*. It's been like this for

ages. Minor incident with a mouse way back when. Got a bit too eager, I suppose." He snorted loudly, then, embarrassed, covered his beak with a wing. "Anyhoo, it's not that big a deal. It's just that ever since, my navigation has been a bit off You know what they say—steer with the ear! And my ears are, well, you know." Otto flopped his wings every which way to illustrate his twisted sense of direction.

Dawn surveyed the rocky terrain, littered with tree stumps and stones. "But why were you flying so low?" she inquired. She shifted her gaze toward the vast open sky above. "It's much safer up there."

Tobin nodded vigorously. "Yes," he agreed. "Flying down here is an accident waiting to happen! Especially with your...condition." Tobin raised a paw to his mouth. "Oh goodness," he uttered. "I'm sorry. I didn't mean any offense."

"None taken," said Otto. "You're correct—absolutely correct. I never fly at this altitude. Only a worm-brain would do something like that. But under these circumstances?" The bird kicked some ash off his foot, exposing his long, orange toes. "Well, I certainly couldn't fly *high*. I shouldn't be flying at all!"

Tobin tilted his head. "Why not? Your sense of direction can't be *that* terrible."

Otto's expression turned suddenly somber. "Because of the beast!" he whispered. "If he sees us, he'll get very upset. This is his territory."

Dawn furrowed her brow. "I suppose that makes sense."

"Well, it should! You were the one who instituted the no-fly zone!"

At this, Dawn's ears pricked up. "Me?" she asked, surprised.

Otto bobbed his head in what must have been his version of a nod. "Oh yes," he replied. "The tuatara said you absolutely forbade it. Flying was far too risky, you told her. Isn't that right?"

Dawn gazed at the horizon. As a gust of wind swept through her fur, her mind raced. Why did Polyphema say the birds were not permitted to fly? That was not what they had agreed to. And why did she say this order came from *her*? The fox narrowed her almond-shaped eyes. This was not sitting right.

"Oomph!" With an awkward hop, Otto adjusted his position so he could see the sun's place in the sky. "Golly gee!" he gasped. "I'd better get back. If Polyphema sees that I'm gone, well, it won't be pretty!" The owl's feathers trembled in the breeze. "She has us on a very strict schedule."

"A strict schedule?" Dawn repeated. The fox hardened her gaze and dug her claws in the ash. "We must get back as well," she announced. Her tone was urgent and tense. "It appears we've been gone far too long."

Chapter Sixteen
THE MISSING BIRDS

"I'm just gonna...stop here...for a moment," huffed Otto. His refusal to fly had made his journey back toward the crater quite a challenge, especially as he tried to keep pace with the swift fox. The owl was breathing so heavily that his breath ruffled his feathers.

"You'll be able to navigate the rest on your own?" asked Dawn.

Otto awkwardly bobbed his head. "Yes," he confirmed. "I'll find my way. Plus, I could use a bit of rest." The owl, normally asleep during the day, let out a long yawn. "The work has been so exhausting."

Dawn gave Otto a nod, motioned to Tobin, then continued her race toward the crater. Without the owl in tow, she could pick up speed and make up for lost time. Soon her trot turned into a run, and before long she had reached the giant hole in the earth. Tobin couldn't keep up with the fox, but he moved as fast as his stubby legs could carry him. He didn't slow down until the crater was in sight.

"Sorry it took me so long," Tobin called breathlessly. He saw Dawn standing at the side of the crater, where the jerboas were furiously weaving the vines into a huge web. They were organized in neat rows and columns so they could work as quickly as possible. As one tiny creature held a strand in his paws, another wrapped it through the next piece so nimbly that it looked like a complicated dance.

Over, under.
Over, under.
Hop, duck.
Hop, duck.

The scene was a sea of floppy ears and reed-like tails. No one stood still, even to catch their breath.

Tobin took a step closer and examined the woven

construction. His beady eyes widened. The jerboas had stayed awake much past their bedtime of dawn and had worked straight through the morning. But despit their exhaustion, they had made impressive progress. The net was almost done. It nearly covered the huge hole in the ground.

"Oh goodness, those poor jerboas!" cried Tobin. "They're working so hard."

Dawn nodded in sympathy, but she was thinking about other things. "Where's Polyphema?" she asked. "And where are the birds?" She stared out at the crowd. The jerboas' constant movement made searching for anyone almost impossible. Finally, she spotted the kiwis at the far side of the net. But the falcons, owls, and hawks were nowhere in sight.

"Hey, you, over there! Back to work! Do you want the beast to turn us all into barbecue?" A sharp voice interrupted Dawn's train of thought, and she spun around in alarm.

It was Bismark. He was perched on top of a rock, shouting out orders, and flourishing his cape to and fro.

"Oh goodness," sighed Tobin. He and Dawn made their way toward their friend.

Upon spotting the fox, a smirk spread across Bismark's face. "Well, well, well," he sang. "If it isn't she-who-thinks-of-me-not."

Dawn took a step closer. "Bismark, we have to regain control here. Polyphema's trying to take over."

"*Regain control*?" Bismark scoffed. "*Mi amore*, can't you see? I'm already in control!" He put his hands on his hips. "I'm in charge of it all. Poly-poo has appointed me maestro!"

Dawn arched her spine.

"*Maestro*?" echoed the pangolin.

"*Maestro* indeed, *mi amigo*. Tutu has recognized my incredible talent and installed me in my rightful place: head honcho, chief glider, Bismark the boss!"

Dawn shook her head. "But Bismark—"

"No time for chitchat," he replied, dismissively waving his flap. "Too much work to do, and these jerboas are slacking off on the job! You there!" he shouted to a team of weavers. "You call that sturdy? *Ridiculo*!"

Bismark hopped off his rock and stormed over to the section of the net in question. He shook his head as he examined the handiwork of the jerboas.

"No, no, no. This won't do. Tutu said it had to be perfect! You've got to pull it tight, *comme moi*." He demonstrated by yanking the vine so hard that it snapped in his hand. "*Mon dieu*! How shoddy! You know what this means?" he asked, waving the torn strands in front of the jerboas' faces. "We're starting over! That's right, the whole pomelo! The entire papaya! Now *vamanos*, get a move on!"

A groan went up from the crowd of jerboas, who had stopped their work for a moment to listen.

"Bismark," said Dawn. She edged close to her friend and tried her best to stay calm. "Where are the birds?"

But Bismark ignored her question. "I'm busy," he said. He pointed at a weaver, who was so tired, he had stumbled away from the net. "To the left, little guy! To the left!"

The jerboa's eyes darted to the glider. Then he meekly lowered his head and trudged back to the net. He could barely lift his feet off the ground.

Bismark looked back at Dawn with triumph. "Everyone *here* sees my true worth—I am a natural-born leader! These animals are drawn to me like moths to a flame. Moths to a flame, I tell you!"

"Listen, Bismark," said Dawn. "This is urgent. Polyphema grounded the birds in my name, and they could be in grave danger."

"Why are you so worried about the birds? Hmm?" Bismark stomped his small foot. "Maybe you should stop worrying about those feather-brained flappers and spend more time focused on yours truly—*moi*—me, me, me!"

"I'm sorry about before." Dawn sighed, trying to push aside her frustration. "Now Bismark, please—"

But the sugar glider was already distracted by another fault in the net.

"Hey, you! You call that weaving? *Mon dieu!*"

"Come on," urged the fox. "Enough of this. We have to go find Polyphema."

Bismark shook his head. "No, no, *muchacha*. My post is here. I have important duties to perform! There's someone new in charge of both the camp and my heart. Someone who wants me as *maestro!*"

"Oh goodness," said Tobin. "I think I should stay, too." He glanced at Bismark then lowered his voice to a whisper. "Someone's got to take care of these jerboas!"

Dawn's gaze traveled over the animals at work. "The birds are definitely missing," she said. "I have a terrible feeling about this." Then she lifted her head and fixed her eyes on a large boulder ahead. A small glimmer, almost like the glow of a moonstone, shone at its top. Polyphema. "There's no time to lose. I must speak to the tuatara at once." Dawn's body stiffened. "Before it's too late."

Chapter Seventeen
HALT!

With her heart pounding hard in her chest, Dawn raced toward the boulder and bounded up its steep side. At the top, perched on a narrow ledge, was Polyphema—front eyes closed, third eye pulsing and twitching.

"What have you done with the birds?" Dawn demanded. She reared up to her full height.

The tuatara winked open a single dark eye. She looked at Dawn, glanced down below at the net, and then closed her eyelid once again. She was in no rush.

Dawn growled. "We don't have time for this! Where are they?"

"Apologies," the tuatara said at last. "My visions cannot be disrupted."

"Where are the birds?" she repeated. "Where have you sent them?"

Polyphema tilted her head. "Why, I've sent them nowhere." She opened her eyes, and Dawn saw them twinkle. "They're here. Can't you see?" The tuatara bent her angular face over the edge of the rock and gestured down toward the net. "They've done a marvelous job. Simply marvelous."

Dawn peered out at the scene below. She could see that work was well underway, despite Bismark's—or Polyphema's—perfectionism. The net's final knots were being tied, and the second layer of vines was starting to be woven in. "Those are the jerboas," she snapped. "I asked you about the—" The fox's voice trailed off. She saw that in certain spots, even where there were no jerboas, the net seemed to be moving as if stirred by an invisible force. But there was no wind blowing. She squinted and saw a tiny orange beak grab the end of a vine, pull it under, and wrap it back around.

Dawn suddenly understood, and the knowledge

hit her like a tidal wave. "They're under the net," she said softly, afraid to believe the words she was speaking. Her horrified eyes met Polyphema's. "*What have you done?*"

The tuatara looked back, unflinching. "I have done what I must," she replied.

Dawn felt her heart pound in her chest. She had to get down there immediately. She had to do something. The fox spun away, but a low chuckle stopped her in her tracks.

"Go ahead." The reptile sneered. "Do your best. Take charge." The tuatara's lips spread in a mocking grin. "No one will listen. Why would they? Why would they defy me when I have the power to see what you can't?"

Dawn slowly took a step back.

"Look at you. You're all alone." Polyphema glanced left and right, and then shrugged. "Even your friends aren't here. How did that happen? Did I steal them away?"

A fire blazed in Dawn's chest. She could feel the burn of anger in her legs, her stomach, her eyes. Every instinct in her body was telling her to pounce. But she held herself back. She could not waste another moment. And so, the fox scrambled down the slope of the rock and raced full-speed toward the crater.

When she arrived, she leaped onto the net, tugging the vines with her teeth, desperate to untie the knots. She heard urgent voices around her, but Dawn shut them out. The fox pulled with all her might. Her muscles tensed, and sweat dripped from her fur, stinging her eyes. But she could not be distracted. She wouldn't stop until the birds were freed.

"HALT!" A group of jerboas shrieked.

The ear-splitting cry filled the air, prompting Dawn to stop at last. The fox wiped her gums with her paw then looked up. She was surrounded.

"What are you doing?" the jerboas shouted in dismay.

"You're ruining all our hard work!"

"We spent all night on those knots!"

Voices rose from under the vines, and there was furious flapping as the birds struggled to push through to the surface. Dawn looked down through the net's gaps and saw a sea of faces staring up at her.

"Move away!" they cried out, joining the jerboas in protest.

"You're wrecking the trap for the beast!"

"Yeah, do you want the beast to win?"

Dawn scanned the crowd, searching for one sympathetic face. Someone who understood. Where were Tobin and Bismark? They must have been there, but there were too many birds and jerboas to see. Their voices grew louder, their protests stronger. She had to do something.

The fox raised her snout to the sky and let loose a guttural howl—*Yoooowwwwwl*—the Brigade's signal for trouble. Alarmed by the noise, the jerboas and birds went silent.

"Listen to me," pleaded Dawn. "I have done all I could to avoid starting a panic, but I'm left with no choice." She wiped the sweat from her brow and held her tail high. "Polyphema does not want your help," she began. With one paw, Dawn pointed down, toward the grid of feathered heads. "She's taken the side of the beast! She wants you gone. This is not a trap for the beast. It's a trap for the *birds*!"

The birds swiveled their heads left and right, squawking in confusion. The impressive seal of the net, the tight knots they had helped tie, the ban on flying—it all suddenly made sense. Their feathers bristled with horror.

Swish. Swish. Swish.

Everyone turned toward the familiar sound of the tuatara's tail sweeping through the ash. They watched in silence as the crowd of jerboas parted, yielding a clear, open path.

With her third eye open, Polyphema swept by

the jerboas, brushed past Dawn, and finally stopped at the edge of the net. Wearing a hint of a grin, she looked down at the birds' feathered heads. "Your so-called leader seems slightly confused," she said evenly. The tuatara glanced sideways at Dawn. "Let me clarify. I never wanted to banish you. The beast did."

"Then why are we down here?" an owl howled.

"Why are we trapped?" screeched a hawk.

Polyphema held a claw to her lips. "You're not *trapped*," she replied. "You're *protected*."

"Don't listen to her," said the fox. "You're not protected. If we capture the beast, you'll be crushed when he falls in the net! Can't you see?"

At this, the tuatara laughed smugly. "No," she hissed quietly. "They cannot. That's the whole point. I'm the only one who can see." Her third eye flashed in the light as she addressed the birds once again. "I know what to do," she insisted. "I know how to deal with the beast. I had to hide you. If you were out here flapping about and he saw you? With the terrible, violent past he has with your kind? Well," she scoffed, "the beast would be *very* upset." The tuatara shifted her gaze from the birds to the jerboas, who had huddled in a nervous cluster. "The beast would destroy all of you!"

The crowd of animals looked at each other,

then at the two leaders before them. Which one told the truth? A tense silence fell over them all.

"Golly gee!" Otto barreled his way through the crowd, wings akimbo, eyes crazed, head unnaturally bent. "Oops," he muttered, accidentally trampling over a jerboa. "Sorry 'bout that. 'Scuse me." After a few more collisions, Otto arrived at the crater's edge. "What'd I miss? Why is everyone so quiet?" He cocked his already twisted head to the side.

"What are you doing out here?" Polyphema bellowed, clawing her way toward the owl. "You need to get under that net—now! Don't you know the beast is coming? Coming for us all!" Desperately, the tuatara reached out, hoping to grab hold of Otto's wing. The crowd stirred, uneasy.

"Come now," Polyphema said, clearly flattening the edge in her voice. "It's for your own protection. And everyone else's as well. If the beast sees you, then—"

"Then what?" challenged Dawn. "What will happen? What do your visions say? And where is this beast you've described?"

But as soon as the words left her mouth, Dawn sensed something strange.

The air felt heavy and charged.

The ground began to tremble below her.

The wind started to blow and quickly turned gusty. It whipped their faces, sending clouds of ash swirling around them.

And then...

BOOM!

Chapter Eighteen
THE BEAST'S ATTACK

"Holy glider!" cried Bismark. "We are under attack! Under siege! We are doomed!"

The animals froze and looked toward the mountain. Low rumbles and violent claps rang from its depths. The ground started to vibrate, hum, and heat up. At first, it felt pleasantly warm, but then it grew uncomfortably hot, threatening to burn their paws. Tiny bits of stone cracked and flaked off in triangles and blew toward the crater.

"It's the beast! It's the beast!" With panicked

cries, the jerboas fled, running as fast as they could back into the forest.

"Oh goodness," moaned Tobin. The pangolin curled in a ball, shielding himself from the stampede of tiny rodents. "Is it true?" he asked, his voice hollow and faint. "Is the beast coming to get us?"

Nervous beads of sweat stained Bismark's brow, but he forced himself to stand tall. "Have no fear, *mi amigo*. The beast is no match for *moi*!"

The sugar glider flexed in a show of strength, but his muscles appeared even punier than usual. Quickly, he tucked them back under his flaps.

The ground jerked violently, and the low rumble from underneath grew louder and louder.

"*Mon dieu*." Bismark shuddered. "Where is Dawn?" Tugging Tobin by the tail, he forged through the sea of jerboas. "Dawn!" he called, pawing his way through the crowd. "*Mon amour*!"

"Bismark! Tobin!"

At the sound of Dawn's voice, Tobin uncurled from his ball and Bismark calmed down. But between the swirling clouds of dust and the dense swarm of rodents, it was nearly impossible to see.

"*Blegh*!" Bismark spat. "This smoke is too heavy and thick, even for my brilliant peepers. He ducked as a sharp, airborne rock whistled over his head. "*Mon dieu*! It's an assault, I tell you! A beastly bombardment! A blitz!"

The earth sizzled and cracked. From the opposite end of the crater, Dawn struggled to maintain her balance. A loud *POP*! rang out near her ear. She heard high-pitched cries, then a muffled wash of beating wings.

"The birds!" she gasped. They were frantically flapping, trapped beneath the expertly woven vines. The ground grew hotter beneath them. Steam rose from the small holes in the net. Panic coursed through Dawn's veins. "We're going to get you out of there!" she called to the birds, unsure if they could hear her over the sounds of chaos.

The fox's eyes darted around, searching for some sort of solution. Then she saw a flicker of light, and a sharp, spiky tail.

"Polyphema!" she yelled. She hated to admit it, but the tuatara's three rows of teeth would be useful in tearing the vines. "Polyphema! Help us!"

But the tuatara was out of earshot—or so it seemed—and she kept moving farther and farther away.

The hair rose on the back of Dawn's neck. While the floppy-eared jerboas and furry kiwis were sprinting away from the mountain where the explosions were loudest, Polyphema was headed toward it, full speed.

"*Mon amour!*"

Dawn spun around, jarred by the sugar glider's high-pitched cry.

"My tawny treasure! My amber ambrosia! My reddish-brown rosebud!" Bismark threw up his paws in pure joy and wrapped himself around Dawn's neck. Tobin, catching up from behind, joined the embrace, nestling his scales in Dawn's fur.

Dawn loosened herself from her friends. "Let's hurry," she said. "We have to remove that net. The birds are still trapped underneath it!"

Bismark widened his eyes in shock. "Are you *loco*, my love? Look around you!" The sugar glider gestured toward the earth, splitting and crackling beneath them. A blast of steam escaped from a gap in the earth, hissing like a thousand vipers. "We have to go! Plus, it might not be so terrible to leave those birdbrains behind." Bismark mischievously stroked his chin. "More airspace for *moi*."

But Dawn was at the edge of the crater, tugging at knots with her already sore teeth.

Tobin eyed the net. He knew it was dangerous, but he could not leave the work to Dawn alone. And he could not leave the birds. "Come on, Bismark," he urged. "We can't abandon the birds. The Brigade leaves no one behind!" Mustering his bravery, the pangolin stumbled toward the fox. Then, using his sharp, pointed claws, he slashed strands of vine, tearing apart the carefully fastened ties.

"Help us!" Below the net, the birds were crying out in despair.

"Hurry!" they shouted. "The beast! He's here! He's attacking!"

Blasts of smoke shot up through the air.

"*Oh mon dieu.*" Bismark groaned. "You'll never untie it in time with those clumsy mitts. I supervised the construction of this net myself!" The sugar glider scampered over the trembling earth toward his friends, and squeezed between them. "Please, *por favor*, allow me. I have just the nimble digits we need." Bismark wriggled his paws then quickly got down to work.

Together, the Brigade pulled, tore, and ripped at the net. At last, with the birds working below and the Brigade working above, one side of it tore wide open.

Like water escaping a dam, the birds rushed from the gap—exiting the crater in a band of multi-colored, soot-stained feathers.

"Eureka!" cried Bismark. He threw his paws

in the air then lowered himself in an exaggerated bow. "Yes, *oui*, you are welcome."

"Freedom!" cried the chorus of birds, unconcerned with anything but escape.

As the earth continued to jolt, the flock, safe in the air at last, flapped away toward the forest.

"*Mon dieu*," Bismark scoffed. "Where is the thank you? The *gracias*? The *merci*? What terrible manners. Those feather-flappers could stand to learn a thing or two from yours truly. Even in the harshest conditions, a glider is always refined."

Tobin squinted up at the birds, then tilted his head, perplexed. "Where's Otto?" he wondered. "Oh goodness, I do hope he's in that flock somewhere."

"Probably not," Bismark sneered. "Those birds are flying successfully—in a *single* direction. That owl-head Otto zigzags worse than a moth in a maze."

Dawn shot Bismark a glare. "I'm sure he's all right," she said. But the fox grew worried as she returned her gaze to the mountain. Steam rose from its peak, and chunks of earth fell from its sides. "Come on," she said. She dug her claws in the shaking ground, struggling to maintain her balance. "We need to leave. Now."

Tobin eagerly waddled toward Dawn, moving safely away from the edge of the crater. Bismark started to follow, but then he paused.

"Ahem! Never fear, *mis amigos*. I can take it from here." Bismark puffed out his chest and dusted the front of his coat. "The birds needed our help, and I obliged—like a true gentleman, I might add—but this brave *muchacho* still has to defeat the beast." He glanced back toward the sputtering crater and the shuddering mountain beyond it. He gulped, but held his ground nonetheless.

"Bismark," said Dawn, "it is too dangerous here." Another quake rattled the earth, and a glowing boulder shot down the side of the mountain. "Don't be silly!"

"*Silly*?" Bismark balked at the word. "I am a sugar glider—airborne wonder, king of marsupials! I am not silly! No, no, no. Nothing, not even the big, bad beast, can defeat—"

A sharp lurch and the tumbling sound of loose rocks drowned out his last word. The land was breaking, fracturing, cracking like the shell of an egg. Solid ground broke into hazardous ledges and jagged trenches. Smoke and heat rose from their depths.

"Whoaaaaaaa!" A zigzagging split pierced the ground just a paw's length away from the sugar glider. On the edge of the newly-formed cliff, Bismark struggled to stay on his feet.

"Bismark!" cried Tobin. "Be careful!"

"Have no fear, *pangolino*!" the sugar glider called, still teetering and tottering over the edge. "I was born equipped for situations precisely like this. Now watch! Learn! Marvel!" He took a deep breath and stood at his full, but still miniscule, height. "This, my friends, calls for the—"

But as Bismark extended his flaps in an effort to maintain his balance, a giant column of smoke burst from the earth behind him.

Dawn's eyes widened. "Bismark—no!"

BOOM!

Propelled by another forceful explosion, a strong gust of ash blew toward Bismark and gathered in his skin-like folds. In less than an instant, the sugar glider's flaps were fully inflated, and he whooshed off the ground like a leaf swept away by a storm.

Dawn and Tobin looked up, searching through the thick smoke and soot for any sign of their friend. But through the ash and the chaos, they could not see a thing. The only trace of the sugar glider was his blood-curdling cry:

"—flaaaaaaaaaaaaaaps!"

Then that, too, faded into the clouds.

Chapter Nineteen
HANG ON, BISMARK!

"I don't see him anywhere!" cried the pangolin. The black, foul-smelling smoke filled his sensitive nostrils and stung his eyes.

"Bismark!" Dawn coughed. "Where are you?"

As if in reply, a shrill cry rang out overhead.

"*Mon dieeeuuuuuu!*"

"Oh goodness!" cried Tobin. Above him, the sugar glider whipped and whirled in the smoke, limbs akimbo, eyes bulging. The pangolin reached up and out with his clumsy digging claws, using his tail to maintain his balance, but his arms were far too short to grab hold of his friend. "What do we do?" he asked Dawn. Panic rang in his voice.

But before the fox could reply, the angry earth seemed to calm. The ground ceased its shaking. The smoke thinned to a wisp, and then faded into the air. Nervously, Dawn and Tobin looked up.

Bismark hung still against the sky, his billowing flaps still full of the rising hot air. "I'm okay!" he yelled. A proud grin flashed on his face as, for a moment, he defied the laws of nature and tasted the sweet nectar of true flight. Then, slowly, his expression shifted to one of pure dread. His ascent slowed, then stopped, and now he was falling downward, faster and faster, right toward a new smoldering split in the earth.

"Use your flaps!" cried the fox.

Desperately the sugar glider tried, flailing and flapping like mad. But it was no use—gravity and time were against him, and, just like that, Bismark vanished into the crack in the ground.

"Bismark?" Dawn yelped. A lump formed in her throat as she anxiously awaited an answer, a sign that he was unharmed.

But nothing came.

For a brief moment, the fox and the pangolin

stood, mouths open in shock. Then, at once, they sprinted toward the deep hole and peered over its edge.

"I…I don't see anything…." Tobin's voice trailed off. All he could make out below were thick swirls of smoke. His stomach tightened with unspeakable dread. He wiped large beads of sweat from his scales—the mouth of the hole was radiating intense heat—then he glanced sideways at Dawn. Her usually calm face was stricken with horror.

"He must be down there," she said.

The fox's mind spun, and her heart felt heavy and pained. What could she do? How could she save her friend? Was it too late?

"The birds!" she exclaimed. "They could help!" But as she squinted through the smoke, she saw that they had already vanished. Thinking quickly, Dawn leaped over the sizzling pockets of earth to the crater a few feet away. Perhaps they could use part of the net to reel Bismark back up to safety. But as she peered over the crater's edge, her stomach sank. The net had already fallen deep into the smoldering pit.

Dawn swallowed hard, trying her best to push away the thought that she might never see Bismark, or hear his voice, or roll her eyes at him, ever again.

"*Dios-mio*! *Mon dieu*!" A high-pitched, familiar

voice rose from the depths of the earth.

The fox's hair stood on end.

"Bismark!" yelped Tobin.

Dawn raced back to the pangolin. They peered into the hole once again. The smoke had thinned, and now they could see Bismark clinging to a narrow ledge with a single paw. The two friends shuddered. The space below the sugar glider was so deep and so dark, they could not even see where it ended.

"This is it!" Bismark wailed. "This is the end! *Il finale! La fin*!" With his free paw, Bismark waved dramatically. His face was crumpled with a strange blend of terror and frustration. "I've always wanted to go out with a bang," he began, "but this was not the way I imagined it!"

Dawn squinted down at the sugar glider. With his arm strained and fatigued and his paw coated with sweat, his grip on the ledge was loosening. "Hold on!" she yelled.

But Bismark shook his head. "It's no use. I cannot." His trembling voice was growing hoarse. "*Hasta luego*, my sweet! Fare thee well, *mon amour*! I shall see you and your tawny tail in another life." And then, with lovelorn eyes and puckered lips, Bismark's paw slipped from its hold, and he tumbled into the deep, deep hole.

And so did Tobin's tongue. Like a giant, pink jump rope, Tobin unfurled it, and it waggled and waved in the depths of the blistering canyon as Tobin aimed it at Bismark, trying to lasso him.

Got him! The sticky surface of Tobin's tongue made contact with Bismark, stopping his rapid fall.

The sugar glider, eyes tightly shut, let out an ear-piercing shriek. "Death has a tongue!" he cried. "I am being swallowed by death!" Bismark squirmed and convulsed, which only resulted in the tongue wrapping even tighter around his body.

Despite his friend's flailing and the sweltering heat, Tobin's tongue held strong. Dawn grabbed hold of his armored body and dragged him backward, and together they reeled in the still-yammering Bismark. The trio collapsed on the ground in a heap.

"Is everyone okay?" gasped the fox.

Tobin slowly rose to his feet. The earth was finally still. "I'm fine," he wheezed. "My tongueth juth a little bit blithtered." He held his tongue in his paws and showed the swollen red lumps.

"*Oh mon dieu!*" Bismark yelped in horror.

"I'm all right, really," said Tobin. "Ith juth a thsmall burn."

"No, no, no." Bismark waved away the pangolin's

words. Then he raised his paw to his own forehead. "I'm not talking about you, *amigo*. I'm talking about me!"

Dawn and Tobin turned toward the sugar glider. Besides a few minor scratches and a thick coat of ash on his fur, he appeared to be completely fine. But then he turned around, exposing a totally singed, utterly hairless rearend.

Dawn and Tobin stared for a moment. Then they erupted in laughter.

"Funny, is it?" snapped Bismark. "Pah!" The sugar glider twisted his torso so he could examine his tiny, bare bottom. "I look *ridiculo*!" he cried, flailing his arms overhead. "Unsightly, *stupido*, stripped!"

"Don't worry, Bithmark," giggled Tobin. "You thstill look—*ow*!" The pangolin winced and raised a paw to his mouth.

Bismark patted his friend on the back. "Yes, *mi amigo*. I suppose you and your lasso of a tongue speak the truth—I still look handsome, indeed."

Dawn sidled next to the sugar glider and looked at his big, brown eyes. "I'm sorry you were hurt, Bismark. We should have stuck together."

Bismark's ash-covered face spread into a grin. "No worries, *ma chérie*. My rear is like my heart, burning forever with love for you! I see your love clearly now—you cannot live without me." The sugar glider sighed blissfully. "Neither fire nor fumes, crest nor crater, fortress nor foe shall ever come between us!"

Dawn lowered her snout and smiled down at her two loyal friends. "Yes," Dawn agreed. "The Brigade stays together." For a moment, the fox relished the moment of peace and camaraderie. Then the wind picked up, and she lifted her gaze toward the forest. "Come," she said, already starting to move. "Let's go check on the others. We must make sure they are safe from the beast."

Chapter Twenty
BLOOD AND FEATHERS

"Oh, thank goodness they're here," said the pangolin. He lumbered over a log toward the group of jerboas and birds. They were clustered together, a sea of feathers and fur beneath the wide canopy of an ancient tree. Even though the worst was over, they still shook and shuddered in fear. "Is everyone all right?" Tobin asked.

At the sight of the Brigade, the animals seemed to let out one big sigh. But their relief was short-lived.

133

Almost immediately, they began to panic.

"The beast! The beast!" the jerboas exclaimed.

"Is he there?"

"Is he gone?"

"Did you see him?"

"Did he follow you?"

Dawn cleared her throat, hushing the anxious crowd. "We did not see the beast," she began. "Let's all remain calm. Remember, the most important thing is everyone's safety. No one was badly hurt, correct?"

The animals murmured and nodded in agreement. With the exception of a few scratches and bruises—and a few minor burns on the birds—they had escaped from the chaos unharmed.

"Good," said Dawn. With the crowd having quieted some, her voice was steadier—more commanding. "Now, are all creatures here?"

"Yes." The jerboas squeaked, the kiwis chirped, the falcons nodded, and the hawks squawked, confirming that their groups were complete. But the owls continued to rotate their heads, unsettled.

Tobin looked at them with concern. "Is someone missing?" he asked. The pangolin started to pad toward the flock, but Bismark yanked his friend back by the tail. "Bah," he scoffed. "They're all here. Those owls just can't keep their heads screwed on straight. The only thing missing here is the fur on my better half!" The sugar glider spun around, presenting his bare rear end to his friend.

But despite Bismark's antics, Tobin's attention remained fixed on the owls. The round, puffy birds were still looking around wildly, swiveling their heads and nervously hooting among themselves.

"It's Otto!" the pangolin gasped. "I don't see him—he's missing!"

"You're right," said the fox, drawing a breath. "We need to find him right away."

"Fret not, *mes amies*." Bismark waved a flap in dismissal. "Have you forgotten how Otto flew? That cockeyed owl has probably zigzagged himself to the northern brambles by now!"

"Otto is a little unpredictable, so perhaps you're right," reasoned Dawn, "but we need to track him down to be sure." She spoke to the crowd. "Our best bet is to return to the crater—that's where we saw him last. Let's go." The fox started to leave.

"But the beast!" cried a kiwi. "What about the beast?"

"Yes," agreed a falcon, flapping his way toward the fox. "We can't fly until that beast is gone!"

"And now our net is torn," lamented a hawk.

The fox stopped and turned back. "We'll take care of the beast," she said. "We'll study the net's damage and repair it as best we can. Everyone will be safe," she said, hoping that she could keep her promise.

Reassured by their leader, the animals followed Dawn back toward the crater. The jerboas skittered through the thick ash and the birds half-flapped, half-walked their way behind the rest. Most were still afraid to fly and anger the beast.

"When will my bum's handsome hairs re-emerge?" Bismark moaned. The sugar glider was walking backward to hide his burnt rear from Dawn. "I cannot bear such a furless existence. What will I do? How will I sleep on those long, chilly days? My tuckus will freeze!" The sugar glider raised a woeful flap to his forehead.

The crowd let out a loud gasp.

"Tragic, *oui*. I know," said the sugar glider.

"No, Bismark. Look!" Dawn pointed to a pool of dark, red blood on the ground. Scattered here and there were damp, matted brown feathers.

"No!" cried Tobin. He rushed over and picked one up with his claw. Fighting back tears, he inspected it, hoping his conclusion was wrong. The pangolin's shoulders slumped; the feather's owner was clear: "Otto."

"You're sure?" asked Dawn. "It's his?"

Tobin nodded.

"He was attacked!" called a hawk.

"Kidnapped!" squawked a falcon.

"Maybe worse…" cried an owl.

The birds shouted and trembled, shaken by anger and fear.

Suddenly, a low, flat voice interrupted the chaos. "I see the beast has left his mark again."

Polyphema emerged from the mountain's long shadow. Her golden irises seemed to shine even through the curtains of dust that lingered in the air.

"All this pain and destruction…." The tuatara picked up a bloody feather and shook her spiky head. "I told you, the beast won't stop unless you listen to me. You won't *survive* unless you listen to me." Her third eye burst open.

The jerboas released ear-splitting squeals, and the birds flapped in place.

"What do we do?" screeched a hawk. "The beast is out there!"

"Out there and angry!" added a falcon.

"We need to trap him!" cried the jerboas. "We

need to repair the net now!"

Despite their fatigue, the animals raced toward the crater, full-speed.

"We have to start right away!" they exclaimed. "Prepare your paws! Ready your beaks! We have no time to—"

But as the animals peered into the gigantic hole in the earth, they fell suddenly silent. The net had burned to cinders, glowing like a fiery spider's web.

"*Mon dieu*! It is hopeless!" wailed Bismark, wringing his tiny paws. "We'll be the beast's midnight mincemeat!"

"No...we'll fix it..." Dawn started. "We'll—"

But the tuatara scoffed, cutting her off. "We have no more time," she said coldly. The spikes on her back seemed to shine. "Otto was the beast's final threat."

"Final threat?" Tobin gulped. "What did the beast do to him? How can we save him?"

"It's too late for Otto," snapped Polyphema. She was shaking now, as if overcome with panic and fury.

"What do we do?" asked a kiwi.

Everyone started shouting at once.

"We have no net! How can we trap the beast with no net?"

"Look at what happened to Otto. We're next!"

"The beast will roast us and have us for dinner!" they cried.

"Everyone—quiet!" Polyphema raised a claw, silencing the crowd. All eyes turned to face the tuatara. In the dim light of dusk, her scales shimmered like crystal. "There is only one thing to do," she announced.

"What is it?" asked the jerboas.

"We'll do anything," added the birds.

For a moment, the fear on Polyphema's wrinkled face gave way to something else, something commanding, something almost calm. "We give the beast what he wants," she explained. The tuatara paused. When she spoke again, her voice pierced the air like sharp ice. "We banish the birds."

Chapter Twenty-One
BANISHMENT

For a single, charged moment, a stunned silence fell over the crowd. The only sound was the wind whistling through the valley.

Bismark leaped next to Polyphema and stroked her scaly cheek. "Come now, Tutti-Fruity," he sang, laughing nervously. "You must have misspoken. The only thing banished around here is banishment itself, *oui*?" Bismark anxiously hopped from foot to foot, waiting for the tuatara to take back her words. But she didn't, and her expression remained distant and stiff.

At last, her thin lips parted. "As I said," she began, speaking in a low hiss, "we have no other choice. Our net is ruined. And the beast will strike again." She lowered her chin toward the ground, exposing her flickering third eye. "He is enraged. I see it."

A low growl arose from the crowd. It was Dawn. Her claws dug into the ground, her jaw clenched tight, and her fur stood up along her back. "Even if you do see something," Dawn started, "banishment is not a choice. Nothing has changed. No one supports you."

The animals began to stir. The birds' feathers trembled with fear and anxiety, and the jerboas chattered nervously among themselves.

Dawn snarled again, this time exposing her long, gleaming fangs. "Give up, Polyphema. You're outnumbered."

The jerboas' chattering grew louder and more ordered, as if they were starting some sort of chant.

Dawn craned her neck, attempting to make out their words, but the wind carried their voices away. Nevertheless, the fox stood tall, encouraged. "The animals are united!" she shouted at Polyphema. "Even without the net, we'll find a way to fight the beast!"

The tuatara flashed a toothy grin. "United, yes,"

she whispered. "With you? No."

Dawn opened her mouth to respond, but before she could speak, the wind slowed its speed and the chanting grew louder, allowing the jerboas' words to reach her ears at last. The fox froze.

"Banish the birds...banish the birds...."

The words, though faint, stuck her like porcupine quills. An unpleasant tingle ran down her spine. The jerboas were not shouting in protest—they were chanting in support.

"Banish the birds! Banish the birds!"

The chant continued, picking up volume and power like an avalanche.

"BANISH THE BIRDS! BANISH THE BIRDS!"

The jerboas were in a frenzy now, jumping up and down, pumping their tiny fists in the air. The birds, meanwhile, retreated, taking the first few steps back in a slow, painful exit. Their faces were blank.

"Oh goodness!" cried Tobin, edging closer to Dawn. "The jerboas are revolting! What do we do?"

"Allow me," Bismark said, cracking his knuckles. "This teensy-weensy little problem will be resolved in no time at all. These little pea-brains forgot who they're dealing with." The sugar glider cleared his throat and cupped his paws to his mouth. "Jerboaaaaaaas!" His voice boomed over the crowd. "This is your *maestro* speaking! Now listen up! *Écoutez!* Lend me your big floppy ears!" Bismark paused and cocked his head. His face crinkled up with confusion. "*Uno momento*," he whispered, glancing over his shoulder at Dawn. "What, exactly, am I commanding these peewees to do?"

The fox marched forward. "Stop your chanting at once," she ordered, narrowing her dark, amber eyes.

"*Exactamente*!" Bismark bellowed. "My words precisely! Stop your chanting! At once!"

But the chanting did not stop. It grew louder.

"BANISH THE BIRDS! BANISH THE BIRDS!"

"*Mon dieu*! Don't you listen to your *maestro* anymore?"

"We're…we're sorry," stammered a jerboa, stepping forward and approaching the Brigade. "We don't mean any disrespect. We just don't have a choice. If we don't banish the birds…well…"

"It's them or us!" another jerboa chimed in. "Either they leave or we die! Banish the birds! Banish the birds!" He raised a clenched paw in the air and picked up the chant.

Step by step, the birds backed away from the

144

angry, wild mob. But then, one hawk sprang forward. "This isn't fair!" he protested. Though his voice came out strong, his speckled feathers were trembling. "We're in danger, too. We worked just as hard as you did to make that trap. We don't deserve this!"

"We wove the net—not you!" the jerboa shot back. "And you're the ones who broke it! If the beast strikes again, we'll be doomed. At least you can escape— you have wings!"

"That's right," said Polyphema. Slowly, she moved forward to stand alongside the fox. "The birds must depart. It would be selfish of them to stay."

Faced with the intimidating glare of the tuatara, the hawk tucked his beak toward his chest and backed off.

"But this is our home!" screeched a falcon. "This is where we were born, where we built our nests, where we lay our eggs!"

The tuatara tightened her muscles and swallowed hard. "The forest has spoken," she declared. "You must leave. Now."

The birds bowed their heads, and the jerboas' chant faded. It was no longer necessary. The decision was made. Then, from the back of the crowd, burst loud, uncontrollable sobs.

"I can't go!" blubbered a kiwi. "I just can't!" She buried her long, pointed beak in her partner's feathers. "Honey, do something! Anything!" The bird was quivering uncontrollably.

Many of the kiwis that surrounded her had begun to shed tears as well.

"*Mon dieu*," Bismark sighed. "I never thought I'd say this—but this is even sadder than losing my fur! Poly-poo," he called, "*por favor*! There must be a better way!"

But the sugar glider's call seemed to fall on deaf ears, for the tuatara simply brushed by him. With measured strides, she wove through the crowd, carving a path with her tail, until she reached the bereaved kiwi birds.

"Oh goodness," said Tobin. "I hope she doesn't get angry. Those kiwis can't take anymore!"

With a knot in her gut, Dawn watched Polyphema. Her heart rate began to quicken.

The tuatara stood before the kiwis, craning her scaly neck, as though she were examining the round, fluffy birds. Then she spoke. The kiwis can stay," she said abruptly.

Polyphema's words struck Dawn like a lightning bolt. While the kiwi birds rejoiced and the other animals buzzed with confusion, the fox was already deep in thought.

"I don't understand," said the pangolin. "Why did she change her mind? Why only the kiwis? Why can't the other birds stay?"

"It's befuddling, indeed," agreed Bismark. The sugar glider scratched the bald spot on his head. "If anything, the kiwis should be banished *first*! Poor excuse for a bird, if you ask me. They can't even glide!"

Dawn's face lit up. "That's it," she breathed. "She's only banishing birds that can fly!"

Tobin looked blankly at Dawn.

"Don't you remember what Otto told us?" she asked. "He said that the birds had been grounded—that Polyphema ordered them not to fly because they were in the beast's territory." The fox paused, lost in thought again.

"*Uno momento*!" called Bismark. "What about me, Tutu? Can't you see with those three eyes of yours? Does this not look like flying to you?" Bismark stretched out his flaps to catch a breeze and lifted from the ground. "Aren't you forgetting to banish the sugar glider?"

"Bismark!" yelped Tobin. Reaching up with his claw, the pangolin pulled his friend back down. "What are you doing? Don't you know what that means?"

The sugar glider's eyes widened with sudden understanding. "Yes," he said. "Yes, of course. Best to keep my brilliant flying abilities hidden for now, I suppose, *oui*?"

Together, the Brigade looked out at the sorrowful sea of feathers. All they could do was watch as the hawks, owls, and falcons walked away, holding each other for strength, and dragging their feet through the ash.

"Isn't there anything else we can do?" Tobin whispered. "Is it really ending like this?"

Dawn placed a paw on her friend's scaly back. "Of course, we'll do something," she said. The fox narrowed her amber eyes and fixed them on Polyphema. "We just need a plan. This isn't the end. Not at all."

Chapter Twenty-Two
THREE GASHES

"So long, sweet birdies." Bismark gave them a quick wave. "I shall think of you as I command the cool, midnight skies."

Tobin stroked the smooth skin of his belly and watched, glassy-eyed, as the birds slunk away. "My tummy's all tied up in knots," he moaned.

"Wait a tick, amigo. It's fear—not grief—that sets off that stinker of yours, *correctamundo*?" Bismark's eyes nervously traced their way from Tobin's stomach to

149

his rear. "*Si*? *Oui*? Right?"

The pangolin nodded…but then his face suddenly crumpled and his eyes shone with alarm. "Look out!" he cried.

The sugar glider's eyes bulged and he plugged his nose with both paws. "*Mon dieu*!" he exclaimed. "I thought you said the coast was clear…not that your stench was near!"

"No," said the pangolin, "I mean, duck!"

At once, the Brigade-mates dropped to the ground.

Whoosh!

Whee!

Zoom!

Dawn looked up, recognizing the uneven flight rhythm. "Otto!" she gasped. "He's alive!"

But the fox's relief quickly turned to concern— something was off in the owl's usual bumblings. This time, his looping and lurching was punctuated with sharp yelps and groans.

"*Mon dieu*!" Bismark cried. "And we thought he was off-kilter *before*!"

The animals eyes darted to and fro, tracking the owl's irregular movements, until he plummeted down to the ground, landing in a puff of feathers and dust.

"Oh goodness!" yelped Tobin. "Are you okay?"

Panting and groaning, Otto staggered to his feet. His eyes were blurry, his feathers were messy and matted, and he swayed back and forth like a reed. Slowly, his beak fell open. "Gollllly geeeee…" he uttered. Then, suddenly, he collapsed, falling facedown to the earth.

"Otto!" cried Tobin.

A falcon at the rear of the departing birds spun around. "Did you say 'Otto'?" he asked. The others quickly chimed in:

"Otto?"

"The owl?"

"He's back!"

The rest of the flock came to a halt. Upon hearing of Otto's return, they sprinted back to camp.

"Move aside!" they cried out. "Let us through!"

Anxiously, the birds pushed through the swarm of jerboas and past the Brigade. When they reached the owl, they erupted in horrified cries. Otto's back was bloody and torn, and along his spine, where feathers had previously bloomed, was a long, violent gash.

"The blood!"

"The horror!"

"The pain!"

The falcons squawked, aghast. The owls spun

their heads backward, unable to bear the sight. Others, however, drew closer to tend to the injured bird. A hawk cradled Otto's head in his wings while a falcon clasped the owl's long, orange talon in his own. And yet another bird, using the tip of his wing, began to wipe away streaks of blood so the group could inspect the wound. But he froze at the sound of a loud, gritty call:

"Everyone! Step aside!"

The group turned abruptly, stirring the dust on the ground. As it settled, Polyphema came into view. Slowly, with measured strides, she made her way toward the owl and examined his torn back.

The tuatara turned toward her audience and dramatically lifted her chin. "It's the mark of the beast!" she announced.

The crowd released a chorus of terrified yelps.

"I warned you," she said. "I told you the beast would attack!"

"What did he do to Otto?" shrieked a hawk.

Polyphema took a step backward, leaving Otto alone, front and center. He had begun to stir. "Ask Otto," she urged. "He has witnessed the beast's wrath himself."

Immediately, the animals closed in around the injured owl.

"Careful!" said Dawn. "Give him space!"

But the animals didn't listen; the frenzy could not be stopped, and they continued to move in closer, until Otto was completely surrounded.

"What did he look like?" they demanded.

"Did he speak?"

"How'd you escape?"

Otto blinked, alarmed at all of the questions, and struggled to get his bearings. Then, slowly, he rose to his feet. His body was trembling—and despite the dryness and heat, his feathers were cold and damp. "G-goll... golly gee! I don't know! Hard to see or hear much of anything with my, well, you know...situation." The owl gestured toward his crooked neck. "Can't really swivel to see what's behind me. But I do know this," he continued. "Something—someone—wanted me dead. I was attacked!"

At this, the jerboas erupted in ear-splitting squeals. The birds frantically flapped in place. Otto shuddered and hugged himself with his wings.

"You heard him," Polyphema warned the terrified birds. "The beast is still out there. Out there and angry! You all need to leave—*now*."

Otto looked down and plucked a loose, bloody feather from his side. "Silly Otto," he muttered. "Clumsy, dotty, featherbrained fool. If not for this kooky neck of mine….” He sighed. “I’m an easy target. What was I thinking, flying at a time like this?”

“Yes, *si*, it’s true.” Bismark nodded. Then he smoothed his fur and stood tall. “A physically perfect specimen such as myself would never have this sort of trouble. No bulls-eye on my beautiful back.”

“This could have happened to anyone.” Dawn shook her head in dismay.

“That’s right!” yelled a falcon. “It could’ve been one of us!”

“It *will* be one of us!” screeched a hawk.

“Yes, it will,” confirmed Polyphema. She bowed her spiked head toward Otto. “Your friend here was spared. He’s lucky to be alive. But—” she paused dramatically, “there’s no telling what the beast will do next.”

“She’s right,” said a hawk.

The owls swiveled their heads in a panic. “Hurry!” they yelled. “Let’s go!”

In a frenzied rush, the animals began to scatter.

“Wait!” yelled the fox.

But no one heeded Dawn’s call. Instead, consumed by their fear, the birds tugged their friends by the feathers, urging them to move faster, and stumbled off toward the trees.

"Poor birds," lamented the pangolin. "Poor Otto!"

The fox shook her head at the departing birds. Then, she shifted her gaze to Otto. With a path finally clear, Dawn made her way to the injured owl's side and leaned over his ragged back. Gently, using her paws, she peeled back his blood-soaked feathers and examined the gash. The fox's almond eyes narrowed to slivers.

"Wait a moment," Dawn said.

"What is it, my sweet?" Bismark asked. "Is it the blood? Are you feeling faint? Shall I hold you?" Without waiting for a reply, the sugar glider ran to the fox and embraced her rear leg.

"Golly gee." Otto winced. "Is it that bad?"

"Not *bad*..." replied Dawn, though the wound was, indeed, deep. "It's just...strange...curious. Look," she said, summoning Tobin. "Do you see? Look at the mark the beast left."

The pangolin stepped next to the fox and bent over Otto. "Oh goodness," he gasped. "There are three gashes!" With his snout, he gestured toward the trio of vertical slashes.

Dawn leaned closer. "Yes. But what's really odd is that they're not solid lines."

Tobin cocked his head and squinted his beady eyes. Dawn was right: each scratch was actually made

155

of several smaller marks. The two outer lines were fairly faint, and the wounds were relatively shallow. The source of most of the blood was the bigger, deeper punctures that made up the center line.

"These marks weren't made by a claw," Dawn concluded.

"Well done, my sleuthy sugar plum ! Well done. Well observed." Bismark eyed the gashes and shuddered. "*Mon dieu*! Whoever did this was really out for blood." He choked back a retch and turned away before Dawn could notice his nerves. Then he looked up at the orange disk of the sun perched high in the blue sky above. "Say… it's getting late in the day, *amigos*, and we've been awake far too long! How about we take a small snooze before we continue this nauseating—I mean, noble— journey? It might be too late for our beat up, broke-neck owl friend here, but I still need my beauty sleep. We are nocturnals, after all."

"This pattern…" Dawn mused, still fixed on Otto's wounds. "It's so…familiar." The fox furrowed her brow and bent closer. "Where have I seen it before?"

"Come along now, my smart *señorita*. Look at something more pleasant." The sugar glider framed himself with his paws. "My handsome face, for example? Or perhaps my *terrifico* tail?" He winked.

The fox looked up with a start. "That's it!" she gasped.

Bismark beamed. "My tail? Fine choice, *mon amour*!"

"Polyphema—"started Dawn. "Where is she?"

The pangolin searched the area. To his left were the departing birds, slumping away toward the sun. To his right were the jerboas and kiwis, buzzing and bumbling with fear. But Polyphema was nowhere in sight. "She—she was just here..." stammered Tobin, bewildered.

The sugar glider stood on tiptoe. "Poly-pee?" he called. "Poly-poo?"

"There!" said the fox. Dawn narrowed her eyes. Polyphema was bolting toward the mountain, full-speed. And in the light of the rising sun, the tips of the spikes on her tail were shining—gleaming—in a deep, dark shade of red.

Chapter Twenty-Three
GOLLY GEE!

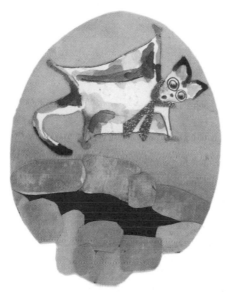

"Stop!" Dawn's voice rang out to the birds who were marching off toward the trees. "Everyone—come back!"

The owls, falcons, and hawks spun around with a start, jarred by their leader's forceful cry.

"What about the beast?" screeched a hawk. "Don't we need to leave?"

Dawn shook her head. "There is no beast! Polyphema's been lying to all of us...and now there's finally proof." The fox's eyes darted after the tuatara just in time to see her long, spiky body slip past the dark, jagged edge of the mountain. "I can't explain now, but she's behind all of this. We have to go! Follow me!"

Without another word, Dawn dashed forward full-speed, urging her friends to follow.

At first, the birds hesitated, but then they started to stir. "We've got nothing left to lose," reasoned a falcon.

"Where else were we going to go anyway?" asked a hawk.

"That's right, birdbrain!" called Bismark, cupping his paws to his mouth. "If any of you featherweights want to stay in the valley, you'll follow that fox!"

Bismark's words kicked the crowd into action. But while the jerboas formed a quick-moving pack behind the sprinting glider and the pangolin, the birds of prey lagged in the dust, tripping over their talons.

"Oh goodness!" cried Tobin. "The birds can't keep up! Dawn, slow down!"

"There's no time to spare!" Dawn shouted, running, her legs churning up the dirt. She had to keep track of the slinky tuatara. "You have to fly!"

The birds nervously glanced toward the skies.

"Fly!" Dawn repeated. "Trust me!"

"I'm trying, my love!" Bismark sputtered, his

flaps waggling pathetically in the ash. At last, his small body rose a paw's length off the earth. "There! I've done it! Tell me you saw that, si?"

"Oh Bismark, she means the birds, not you!" Tobin cried. "Come on, birds! We need to stick together. You have to trust us!"

"But flying is dangerous!"

"That's what got Otto attacked!"

"GOLLLYY GEEEE!" Otto interrupted with a sudden squawk and a burst of wings. "There's no time for this. Let's follow the fox!"

Encouraged by Otto's brave battle cry, the flock of birds rose in a magnificent wave of brown, gray, and gold. Together, they flew closely behind the land animals, their feathers aglow with the afternoon light.

Tobin hurried to catch up. His eyes widened as he realized they were going around the mountain—to the fortress.

Dawn stopped when the tower of rocks was in sight. "Everyone, hush," she whispered, placing a paw to her lips.

"What's that *mon amour*? Hush?" Bismark asked, half-flapping, half-running to catch up to the tuatara. "Don't you mean *rush*? Forward? Charge? Why the hold up?" he huffed. "If there is no beast, as you

161

say—if Tutu-tata is behind all of this—then I say it's go time!"

But despite Bismark's furious flapping, he remained grounded; Dawn was holding him back with her paw.

"We will talk to Polyphema later," she said. The fox fixed her eyes on the fortress. She had a strong hunch that it held the answers to all of their questions. "For now, the best thing to do is just watch."

Silently, the jerboas and kiwis huddled in the shade of a boulder, while the birds of prey—their feathers silent and still—perched overhead on the narrow, raised ledge of the mountain.

"Oh goodness, there she is!" whispered Tobin. With his snout, he gestured toward the fort's outer edge, where Polyphema stood pressed against the stone wall.

The Brigade crept forward. The tuatara was speaking. They could hear her low rasp, but could not make out her words.

Carefully, the fox stepped closer, emerging into the light. Tobin and Bismark tiptoed behind her.

"Shhhh," Dawn whispered. It was risky to be this close. If Polyphema turned, the Brigade would be in plain view and her entire plan would be ruined. But the determined fox crept even closer to the tuatara. Finally, at just a tree's length away, she stopped. Dawn craned her neck and her ears pricked up.

At last, the reptile's words became clear. "*I will protect you.*"

"Who is she protecting?" asked Tobin.

Bismark leaped in front of his friends. "Um, *excusez-moi, mis amigos*, but the real question is what is Tutu doing *talking to a rock*?" The sugar glider scoffed. "This explains everything. This whole time, Poly-poo poo has been Poly-cuckoo. Cuckoo! Cuckoo!" Bismark began to spring up and down in the ash, waving his flaps like a fiend. "Crazy! Crazy! Cuckoo! Cuckoo!"

Then, abruptly, he stopped as the fox glared at him with a searing mixture of anger and disbelief.

"Cuck...oops?" Bismark sheepishly covered his mouth.

But it was too late. The sugar glider had revealed their position and, at once, the tuatara spun to face the Brigade. "What are you doing here!" she hissed. But before anyone could reply, she began to look around in a frenzy. "Where is everyone?" she demanded. "Did the birds leave?"

Bismark scrunched his tiny face. "What's going on here, Poly? Hmm? You're all loopty loo."

"I asked you a question!" The tuatara's voice was

uncharacteristically loud, high-pitched, and panicked. "Where are they? Where are the birds?"

"Oh goodness," said Tobin, confused. "Can't you see? They're right above your third eye!"

For a moment, Polyphema froze. Her jaw tightened; the scales on her face turned pale. Then, slowly, she tilted her head to look up... with her two front eyes.

The tuatara gasped. So did the Brigade.

"*Mon dieu*!" Bismark shook his head side to side. "That three-eyed Tutu is a two-faced fraud!"

Dawn approached the reptile, exposing a gleaming, white fang. "You don't see anything out of that eye," she snarled, peering into the dull, milky orb. "Not the birds, not the beast, not anything! There is no special 'sight.' There is no sight at all. There is no beast!"

The birds above let out a gasp.

"Look!" Dawn continued, beckoning Otto. The fox led the injured owl toward the dumbstruck tuatara, then she positioned them back-to-back. His three, dotted wounds perfectly matched the three ridges of spikes on the reptile's tail.

"She is the one who attacked Otto!" Dawn blared. She pointed to the dark, caked blood that stained Polyphema's scales. "*She* is the real beast!"

164

Chapter Twenty-Four
DOWN, DOWN, DOWN...

The afternoon air filled with the screams and squawks of the horrified animals.

"But why?" they cried. "Why would you do this to us?"

Polyphema took a step back.

"Yes, why?" asked Tobin, shaking his snout in dismay. "Oh goodness, what do we do with Polyphema now?"

"Nothing—" started the fox.

"Nothing? *Nada*? Zilch?" Bismark cut off his friend and raised his flaps in disbelief. "This traitorous Tutu must pay!"

"Nothing *yet*," finished Dawn. "First, we're going to find out what's in that fortress."

"NO!" The tuatara released a terrified scream. "I mean…no." Though she lowered her voice, it still rattled with panic. "That's not necessary. There's nothing else to see. I confess! It was me—I am the beast!" Polyphema hurried forward and bowed before the Brigade. "Take me away," she urged. The tuatara shot a quick, nervous glance over her shoulder at the fortress. "*Now*!"

"Not until we see what you're hiding," said Dawn.

As the fox brushed past the reptile, Polyphema began to shudder. But then, so did the ground.

"Oh no!" Tobin gasped. Rocks and pebbles trembled near his paws. "The beast is striking again!"

The other animals cried out, too. "The beast! The beast!"

"He's back!"

"Run away!"

"Ha! Silly animals…." Bismark chuckled. "You're forgetting what you just learned! Polyphema just told us there is no beast." The earth lurched under

Bismark's feet, knocking him down to his rear. "But wait *uno momento*...." The sugar glider scratched his bald spot and swiveled toward Polyphema. "If there's no big, bad beast—if all this was you...then how is the earth still shaking?"

The tuatara's eyes darted from animal to animal as they closed in around her. "Okay...I'll tell you," she stammered. "But then you must leave my fortress alone."

The earth gave a sharp jolt and the animals shrieked in terror.

"Oh goodness, the rumbling is growing stronger!" The pangolin tried to grip the earth with his claws. He looked pleadingly at Polyphema. "Please tell us what's going on! Who's doing this?"

"Tell us *now*," growled Dawn. The fox snarled, baring her glistening, white fangs.

"It's not a question of 'who,'" said the tuatara. "The shaking isn't from any animal. It's from the earth itself. This peak—" the tuatara flicked her spiky head up, "—it's no ordinary mountain. It's a volcano."

"A vol-what now?" asked the sugar glider. The ground shook yet again, and Bismark desperately clung to Dawn's leg.

"It's a mountain that opens down toward the

167

earth's core. When pressure builds up underground, it blows up. The land shakes, and rocks and smoke shoot through the air."

The volcano grumbled and moaned. The animals looked up to see stone and ash burst from the mountain's top.

"It's true…" observed Tobin.

Polyphema nodded vigorously. "Yes, I've told you the truth. Now, even if just for your own sake, leave!"

The volcano rumbled again, spitting up more hot debris. Rocks began to tumble down the steep slopes.

"It's too dangerous!" cried a kiwi. "Let's go!"

"Run!" squealed the jerboas.

"Fly!" squawked the birds.

In a panicked swarm, the animals fled, fearing the exploding volcano.

"Come on!" shouted Bismark. "We gotta get out of here!" He tugged at the fox's fur, but Dawn would not budge.

"Just a moment!" she said, shouting over the booms and the blasts. "You haven't answered all of our questions!" The fox ducked, avoiding a falling stone. "What about the print in the crater? The shape of the giant beast?"

"Dawn, it's too dangerous!" exclaimed Tobin. "We'll find that out later—we have to leave!"

"My scaly *amigo* is right," Bismark cried. "We need to get out of here, *pronto*. Never again shall I suffer such a devastating loss!" The sugar glider swiveled his tiny torso and eyed his bare bottom. Then he bolted toward the fortress and clambered up its stone wall. "To higher ground!"

"No, Bismark! Come down!" Tobin's voice rang from below.

"Yes! Come down!" Dawn yelled to her friend. "It's too dangerous up there. We must all stay together!"

"Together?" said Bismark. "You and *moi*?" The sugar glider raised his brows and clutched his paws to his heart. "Say no more, my sweet fox! I'd risk anything for you…even my beautiful fur. I shall fly to you, *mon amour*!"

Bismark beamed. Then, he extended his limbs and began to frantically flap and pump. "*Arriba!*" he squealed. "Watch me soar! A volcano is no match for true love."

Anxiously, Tobin and Dawn observed their friend from below. For a few glorious moments, Bismark remained airborne over the tower. But his flaps were made for gliding on the wind, not for flying, and the sugar glider began to fall down, down, down—down into the hole at the top of the fortress, down into its depths.

Chapter Twenty-Five
LIFE AND DEATH

"Nooooo!" Polyphema screamed, then lunged, full-force, toward the fortress.

But Dawn quickly caught the end of the reptile's tail and yanked it back hard. "You're not going anywhere," she growled.

"Release me!" screamed Polyphema. "Release me at once!"

Dawn held firm, and as she gripped the panicked tuatara, Tobin neared the fort. "Bismark!" he called through the wall. "Are you okay?"

"Oof." The sugar glider opened his eyes and groaned. From his position flat on his back, he could see nothing but tall, dark, stone walls leading up to a small circle of sky.

"Bismark?" the pangolin repeated.

Slowly, the sugar glider rose to his feet. Though the earth had stopped shaking, he still felt off-balance and grabbed onto a rock for support. "D...Did you see that stunning...swan dive?" he called, struggling to speak. "Did you see me...soar?"

"Oh, Bismark, are you hurt?" Tobin asked. "That was a really long fall!"

"Pah! All part of the plan, *mi amigo*." Bismark straightened up, but then winced at the pain in his back. "And, by the way, that was no *fall*! Did you not see my flaps? I *flew* my way down here...and with grace, I might add."

"Then fly out, this instant!" cried Polyphema, still squirming under Dawn's hold. "And do not touch *anything*! Do you hear me? Not a thing!" The tuatara's shrill call pierced the air and echoed throughout the fortress.

"I heard you the first time!" said Bismark, covering his ears with his flaps. The sugar glider spun in a circle, taking in his surroundings. All he could see was dark stone and dirt. What was there to touch, anyway? "There's nothing down here—*nada! Zippo! Zero!*"

Crack.

"Was that my creaky bones?" Bismark wondered when he heard the sharp sound. "I hope I didn't fracture a flap."

"Come on, Bismark," Dawn urged, "look around! Now that you're in there, you can find whatever oho's hiding." Though her hold on Polyphema remained strong, Dawn's paws were already growing tired.

The sugar glider paced around the interior of the fortress. It was small—only ten or so steps across. "*No comprendo...*" he murmured, confused. "What is Poly-poo so afraid of me touching? A little dirt?" Bismark scrunched his nose in disgust as he flicked a large clump off his shoulder.

Crack.

Bismark cocked his head. "That sound again?" The sugar glider looked left and right, but all he could see was the darkness. He shrugged. "I'm telling you, *bella* Dawn, the only thing down here is stone and dirt."

Polyphema nodded vigorously. "Yes, that's right, only dirt! Now get out of there before you ruin that nice fur of yours!"

"*Mon dieu*," Bismark muttered, feeling the dirt caked between his toes and in his ears. "Tutu is right— I'm going to need a new coat after this!"

The fox let out a grunt. The tuatara was wriggling and writhing, still attempting to escape her firm grasp. "It's no use struggling," said Dawn. But her grip was slipping. "We're going to get to the bottom of this, once and for all. We're going to see what you're hiding."

"My sweet, you know I hate to disappoint you, but I think Tutu might be right this time. Cuckoo...but correct," Bismark said, squatting low to the ground. "There is nothing but filth and decay! I think it's time I depart, *mon amour*."

Crack!

"Waah!" Bismark leaped in the air and looked around once again. "Hello? *Hola? Salut?* Is something in here?" The sugar glider trembled as he extended his flaps and blindly groped through the dark. "*Nada*, again," he sighed. But, still curious, Bismark explored the ground. Suddenly, he felt something. Something slimy and wet. "*Blegh*!" he cried.

"Oh goodness, what is it!" cried Tobin.

The sugar glider lifted the small, slippery creature. It writhed in his grip. "A worm!" he grimaced. "One of your favorites, *amigo*." Setting the slimy thing free, Bismark plunged his paws back in the earth, continuing the search. But this time, he felt something beneath the dirt. Intrigued, he tore through the ground until he revealed three small, pale spheres. "What are these?" he mused, scratching the bald spot on his head.

"Did you find something?" called Dawn.

"No! Please!" Polyphema cried. She stopped struggling for a moment and choked back a sob. "Please, stop! Just stop!"

As Bismark tried to brush off the dirt, his eyes widened. "They shine in the light! Hmm...perhaps I can use them to see my reflection and clean myself up." Holding one of the spheres in his paws, the sugar glider angled his body, hoping to view his backside. "Ugh," he grunted. "I can't see a thing through all of this grime! If I could just buff them up a bit...."

Bismark set the orb back down next to the other two. Then, perching over all three spheres, he extended his flaps and furiously began to polish and shine them.

"Just a moment, *amigos*! I'm just taking one last look around," Bismark bluffed. He was still rubbing and shining the orbs. "There's nothing here," he said to himself, continuing to polish. "If I can't find Tutu's hidden treasure then, by the stars, at least I'll come out looking my best!"

The sugar glider moved his flaps faster, struggling to make the spheres shine. "Almost… there…" he said breathlessly. "Almost—"

Crack!

Bismark froze.

Crack!

Crack!

Crack!

The sound was sharper now. Louder.

"What's going on?" Dawn asked urgently. Her ears pricked on end. "What's that sound?"

The sugar glider gulped. "S…something is in here!"

"Oh goodness!" cried Tobin. "What is it?"

Crack!

Crack!

Crack!

Bismark looked around frantically, but there was still nothing to see in the dark.

Crack!

Crack!

CRACK!

At this last loud, splitting crack, Bismark froze and his eyes bulged with horror. He felt something moving…right under his flaps.

Chapter Twenty-Six
UNCLE BISMARK

"*Stop*! Please! Get away!" Outside the walls, Polyphema lunged forward with the last ounce of her strength. Pressing her heels in the ground, Dawn pulled back...but her paws could no longer hold. The tuatara finally broke free and bolted full-speed toward the fortress.

"Get back here!" Dawn shouted. She raced after the tuatara. "Tobin, hurry! We'll catch her before she climbs in!"

But the tuatara made no attempt to scale the fortress's side. Instead, she tightened her jaw, lowered her skull, and barreled straight into its wall.

Crash!

Rocks tumbled down around her like rain and the fortress collapsed, a wave of ash in its wake.

"Bismark!" the pangolin cried.

Dawn and Tobin dashed forward through the shower of pebbles and dust. When the air cleared, the friends froze.

There, in the middle of the half-fallen fortress, Bismark stood over three, tiny, newborn tuataras, breaking free of their shiny, cracked orbs.

"Oh goodness! Bismark!" said Tobin, squeezing past a large rock. "You found—eggs!"

"*Exactamente, mon ami*! I found eggs! The beginnings of life! There was nothing to fear, scaly chum. No big, bad beast hidden in here. Just three mini-Tutus!"

"My babies!" Polyphema shouted. "Get away from my babies!" Sputtering and spitting out ash, the tuatara rose from the rubble and shoved Bismark aside. "Oh Lyla, oh Celtus, oh Galas! You're finally here!" she cooed. "Are you okay? Are you scared? Are you hungry?"

"Wait a second, Tutu. Aren't you forgetting something?" asked the sugar glider. "A *gracias, a merci,* a thank you? Uncle Bismark over here finished hatching those tykes with the heat of these very flaps!"

"Mommy?" peeped one of the hatchlings. "Mommy? Mommy?" echoed the other two.

"Yes!" cried Polyphema. A trickle of blood slowly seeped from just beside her third eye—a wound from her forceful crash into the fortress. Tears streamed down her face. "Yes, yes! I'm your mommy! Mommy's here!"

The babies stared at Polyphema, their tiny eyes lost and confused. Then they looked up at Bismark. "Mommy!" they cried. Together, with outstretched claws and open mouths, the babies reached for the sugar glider. "Mommy, mommy!"

"*Mon dieu!*" Bismark cried. "I said 'uncle,' not 'mama!' This is all tutu much!"

"So this is what you've been hiding," Dawn murmured, joining the group at the nest. She narrowed her eyes at the tuatara. "But why in here? Why all the lies and deceit?"

"*Si!* What's with all the terror, the drama, the cuckoo craziness?" said Bismark. "Why all the hate for the birds, the forest flappers like *moi*?" The sugar glider attempted a glide, but the three newborn babies were fixed to him, clinging to his legs.

"This place was supposed to be safe," began Polyphema. She eyed the remains of the fortress and shook her head. "But then this mountain—this *volcano*—erupted and blew off the tower's top. My eggs were completely exposed from above! All my other children...all my other eggs...they were always eaten by birds!" The tuatara choked back a sob. "What else could I have done!?"

"Oh goodness! That's terrible!" Tobin cried.

"Of course," Dawn breathed. "'Banish the birds.' Banish your natural predators. And now we know why."

Bismark placed his paws on his hips. "Wait, *uno momento*, Poly. Let me get this straight. You wanted to banish ALL flyers, even your trusty *maestro*, just to save a few of your own?"

"You don't understand," Polyphema protested. "I'm nearing the end of my life." She bowed her head. In the slanted, pink light of the dusk, her skin's creases appeared extra dark, extra deep. "These are my final hatchlings!" she cried.

"Oh no..." said Tobin.

"And I'm one of the last of my kind!" she continued. "Tuataras are severely endangered. I *have* to protect my babies... they're my species' only hope!" Polyphema gripped the toppled fortress rocks for support. "Do you want us to end up like that creature you saw in the bottom of that crater? Do you want us to end up *extinct*?"

Upon hearing this dreaded word, Tobin cowered, curling the end of his tail. Even Bismark stood in a rare, serious silence.

Dawn furrowed her brow. "The creature..." she started. "The beast.... Of course!" Her face brightened with understanding. "That shape in the crater—it's a fossil!"

Tobin's beady eyes grew wide. "A fossil?" he repeated.

"Not a skeletal fossil," Dawn explained. "We've seen those before. We've seen enormous bones. This fossil is a different kind. It's an ancient mark of an animal's activity, like walking or resting, captured in stone."

Polyphema nodded. "Fossils like the one in that crater are all that is left of my ancestors. If it weren't for these remains, they'd be forgotten in time and memory."

"Wait a moment," said Tobin, "I've heard of these large, extinct creatures." The pangolin thoughtfully cocked his head. Then his scaly face lit up in awe. "Oh goodness!" he cried. "Are you related to—"

"Unbelievable! *Incroyable*! Insane!" Bismark leaped off the ground, eyes bulging. Tutu! You and your one-two-three mini-Tutus—you're all the descendants of dinosaurs!"

"It's true!" said the reptile. "I am what's left of that ancient race of giants! We once roamed the earth as kings, and now we are forced to hide and cower in ruins." Polyphema held up a fistful of the fortress's crumbling dust. "After the volcano's eruption uncovered the fossil, it was like a vision of the future. A vision of death. I had to do what I did. My species depended on it!"

"Oh goodness," breathed Tobin. The pangolin scratched his scales, trying to take it all in. "So everything—building the net, banishing the birds, even injuring Otto—it was all to protect your family."

Polyphema nodded in sorrow.

The three little hatchlings cocked their heads at the glassy-eyed tuatara. Then, slowly, they wobbled toward her and settled under her chest. Smiling through her tears, Polyphema drew them in close.

A warm, soft breeze filled the air, stirring the ash on the ground. For a moment, Polyphema and the Brigade thought about all that had happened between them since they'd first met by the crater.

"We all want to protect those we love," Dawn whispered, gazing north, toward the brambles. For a moment, she stood in silence, as though traveling back to the past. Then she took a deep breath and turned back to the tuatara. "But no matter what," she said, "we cannot let our fear control us. We must take responsibility for our actions, not invent some beast to take blame."

The tuatara gazed up at the fox. For the first time without anger, the two females' eyes met.

"You're right," whispered Polyphema. "I'm sorry. I'm so very sorry."

Dawn nodded, then she lowered her snout toward the hatchlings. They remained huddled close to their mother, nestling against her scales. "You will not go extinct," said the fox.

The tuatara swallowed hard, struggling to hold back her tears. "What about when I'm no longer here to watch over them?" she asked.

"We will keep them safe," Dawn assured her. "You have my word."

The tuatara gratefully bowed her head. Her third eye had stopped moving and retreated back in its lid, as though it were finally at rest. A moment of peaceful silence fell over them, and then—

"Golly gee!"

The animals spun toward the scratchy, familiar voice that rung from the side of the mountain. Otto's sideways head peered past its jutting edge.

"You can come out Otto," said Dawn. She smiled at the kooky, cockeyed owl. "It's safe now. Safe for everyone."

"Oh...but what about Polyphema?" asked Otto, still shielded by the stone edge.

"It's safe," Dawn repeated. "I promise. Come on over. Polyphema has something to tell you."

"Oh Golly. Golly gee whiz." Nervously, Otto teetered toward the group.

Polyphema swallowed hard and tilted her head sideways to gaze into Otto's golden eyes. Then, slowly, she stepped back to reveal her three, tiny children. "I want you to meet my new babies," she said. "And I want to apologize—to you and your kind. I tried to protect my eggs, but I only succeeded in hurting animals I should have trusted." She paused. "Otto," she started, "I'm so sorry."

"Golly, Poly..." breathed Otto. The owl's eyes shifted from Polyphema to the three newborn babies gathered close by. Gradually, his gaze softened and his tattered feathers relaxed. "I...well, gee whiz."

"Gee whiz?" echoed Bismark. "Don't you mean *three* whiz? Meet my new niece and nephews! But you better not teach them that 'golly gee' habit of yours. I intend for my little Pollies to speak all the languages under the stars as clearly as a moonlit night."

Otto took a few hops closer to the three babies. He lowered his beak and nuzzled them gently. "Well, hiya, there little guys," he said.

Still anxious for the owl's forgiveness, the tuatara shifted her weight and nervously looked at Otto.

"Oh, golly gee," he uttered, meeting the reptile's gaze. "Of course I accept your apology. What cute little kiddies you've got, Poly!"

The tuatara exhaled a sigh of relief and gratefully bowed to the owl. "We will always remember your kindness."

Feeling a deep peace at last, Dawn gazed upon the horizon. A new, glowing moon had climbed into the deep, blue sky. "Come on," the fox said with a smile. "Let's go home. All of us."

Chapter Twenty-Seven
LEGACY

"Goodbye, fort!" Bismark called, glancing back over his shoulder. "*Hasta luego*, volcano! *Adios* big, bad beast!"

As the rest of the group passed the crater, the sugar glider stepped to its edge and eyed the fossil one final time. "Hmm," he mused, cupping his chin in his palm. "No offense, Tutu...but your ancestors weren't exactly the smartest."

Polyphema paused in her tracks, confused. The

three babies were clustered tightly on her back, nodding off as she walked.

"I mean, what kind of fool wants his legacy down here below ground? How shortsighted, silly, *stupide*!" Bismark threw up his flaps, then looked back toward the volcano. His bulbous, brown eyes lit with an idea. "Now *that's* more like it," he said. "Take note, everyone! Listen up!"

The animals turned toward the glider.

"When it's time for *my* fossil—my handsome, forevermore print on this earth—I want it placed *above* ground, *capiche*? Up on the tallest of peaks, for all the world to see and admire!"

Tobin giggled and covered his snout with his claw. Even Dawn cracked a grin.

"What's so funny, *amigos*? I'm sure we can find some space on the mountain for your fossils, too. Under mine, for example."

Quickly, Bismark scurried toward the fox and the pangolin and wedged his way in between them. "Now let's get back to the valley and get some beauty rest! This fur isn't going to regrow itself! You know, Tutu, I'm not so sure I've forgiven you for *that* part of our little adventure." His tail swished over his bare bottom.

Polyphema grinned. Her three young ones were fast asleep. "Personally, Bismark, I think the new bald spot suits you," she said. "It even matches the one on your head."

"*Quoi*? That is *ridiculo*! Who has ever heard such terrible fashion advice?" the glider scoffed. But then he paused. "What say you, *mi bella* Dawn? Does Poly-poo have a point?"

The fox raised an eyebrow and opened her mouth to reply, but then she caught Polyphema's glance and winked. "Sure, Bismark. Very handsome. Don't you like his new look, Tobin?"

"Oh goodness!" Tobin laughed. "Oh, yes, definitely. Bismark, you look wonderful."

"Well, scaly chap, I'm not used to taking style advice from a stink-butt. But if *mi bella* says it looks 'handsome'..." The sugar glider leaped in the air, spread his flaps wide, and spun to show off his bare backside. The three others politely averted their eyes.

"Let it be known!" declared Bismark. "Whoever is in charge of designing my fossil, remember this, and remember it well: when it comes time to imprint my immortal form, make sure that my bottom matches my top!"

Satisfied with his decision, the sugar glider

scurried between Dawn and Tobin and wrapped a flap around each. Then, side by side, surrounded by old friends and new, the Brigade followed the full moon toward home.

THE NOCTURNALS

Bonus Content

*

Character Animal Glossary

*

Discussion Questions for Your Book Club

*

Q&A with Author Tracey Hecht

*

Character Animal Glossary

Falcon
Scientific Name: *Falco berigora*
Common Name: Brown falcon
Physical Characteristics: body length of 41-51 cm with a wingspan of 88-115 cm, reddish brown upper body; with reddish edges to the feathers, and white or cream below with dark streaks on the breast; adult males lightest color and females darkest color; long legs and quite small feet
Behavioral Characteristics: diurnal; mainly solitary; spend considerable amounts of time maintaining their plumage, preening and bathing in dust or water; exceptional eyesight is used to catch fast moving prey
Diet: small mammals, insects, reptiles, birds
Map: species found widespread in Australia and New Guinea
Habitat: tropics, in open rather than forested habitats, and in lowlands rather than at high elevations.
Major Threats: no major threats
Status: Least Concern

Jerboa
Scientific Name: *Euchoreutes naso*
Common Name: Long-eared jerboa
Physical Characteristics: body length of 7-9 cm with tail that is 15-16 cm long; reddish yellow upper body; white belly; tail covered with short hairs and has white or black tuft on the end; hind foot is 4-4.6 cm long and has five digits; ears are one-third longer than head
Behavioral Characteristics: nocturnal; dig burrows; hunt at night; bathe in dust as a form of chemical communication; may use sounds or vibrations to communicate
Diet: flying insects
Map: species found in southernmost Mongolia and regions of northwestern China
Habitat: sandy valleys covered with low-growing bushes; cold, high-elevation desert or semi-arid desert regions
Major Threats: no major threats
Status: Least Concern

Kiwi

Scientific Name: *Apteryx australis*
Common Name: Brown kiwi
Physical Characteristics: flightless bird with wings just 5 cm long; about the size of a chicken; brownish grey with long, soft feathers that look and feel like fur; tough skin; whiskers at base of bill; small eyes with poor vision; no tail; powerful legs; fast runners
Behavioral Characteristics: nocturnal; shy and mainly solitary; build burrows; beat prey on ground before eating it; usually try to escape threats instead of attacking; coil body into a ball when hiding in burrows
Diet: worms, insects, crayfish, amphibians, eels, fruit
Map: species found on islands of New Zealand
Habitat: subtropical and temperate forests and grasslands; prefer large, dark forest areas
Major Threats: predators, such as dogs, pigs, cats, brush-tailed possums and stoats
Status: Vulnerable

Pangolin

Scientific Name: *Manis javanica*
Common Name: Malayan pangolin
Physical Characteristics: covered from just above nostrils to tips of tails by many rows of hard, overlapping, movable, sharp-tipped scales; 79-88 cm long, including the prehensile tail; scales on back and sides are olive-brown to yellow; underbelly and face are white; skin is bluish gray; small, conical heads
Behavioral Characteristics: nocturnal; mainly solitary; timid; climbs trees; moves fast when threatened; strong digger
Diet: ants and termites
Map: species found in southeastern Asia within the Indomalayan regions
Habitat: primary and secondary forests, open savannah country, areas vegetated with thick bush, gardens and plantations
Major Threats: hunting and poaching
Status: Critically Endangered

Owl

Scientific Name: *Ninox strenua*
Common Name: Powerful owl
Physical Characteristics: body length 45-65 cm with wing length 381-427 mm; facial disc is dark brown surrounded by bright yellow eyes with prominent eyebrows, and bluish-horn bill with bristly feathers at its base; males are larger and heavier than females
Behavioral Characteristics: nocturnal, sedentary; nests in tree cavities or the nests of other species; flight is slow and deliberate; prey is often swallowed whole with the fur, feathers, and bones later regurgitated in pellets
Diet: arboreal mammals, large birds
Map: species found in southeastern Australia
Habitat: typically wet and hilly woodlands with dense gullies adjacent to more open forest
Major Threats: no major threats
Status: Least Concern

Red Fox

Scientific Name: *Vulpes vulpes*
Common Name: Red fox
Physical Characteristics: pale yellowish red to deep reddish brown coat on top with white or ashy underside; lower parts of legs usually black, tail has white or black tip, dark brown or black nose; body length is 45.5-90 cm and tail length is 30-55 cm
Behavioral Characteristics: nocturnal; solitary; often live in dens abandoned by other animals; can run up to 48 km/h and jump up to 2 m high; stay in same home range entire life
Diet: rodents, rabbits, insects, fruit, carrion
Map: species located throughout much of the Northern Hemisphere from the Arctic Circle to Central America, the steppes of central Asia, and northern Africa
Habitat: forest, tundra, prairie, desert, mountains, farmlands, and urban areas
Major Threats: loss of habitat
Status: Least Concern

Sugar Glider

Scientific Name: *Petaurus breviceps*
Common Name: Sugar glider
Physical Characteristics: head and body 12-13 mm; tail 15-48 mm; bluish-gray back with pale front; dark stripe down back to end of nose; stripes on side of face; gliding membrane from outer side of fore foot to ankle of rear foot; scent glands on forehead and chest
Behavioral Characteristics: nocturnal; spread limbs to open gliding membrane to glide up to 45 meters; nest in groups; territorial; males mark members of group with scent glands; use sounds to communicate with each other
Diet: pollen, nectar, insects and larvae, arachnids, small vertebrates
Map: species found in New Guinea and certain nearby islands, Bismark Archipelago, and northern and eastern Australia
Habitat: forests of all types
Major Threats: loss of habitat
Status: Least Concern

Tuatara

Scientific Name: *Sphenodon punctatus*
Common Name: Tuatara
Physical Characteristics: body length from about 40 cm to 60 cm; grey, olive, or brackish red in color; lack external ears, possess a "parietal eye or third-eye" on the top of their head which contains a retina and functions like a normal eye, with a scale growing over it in adult tuataras; unlike all other living toothed reptiles, the tuatara's teeth are fused to the jaw bone
Behavioral Characteristics: nocturnal, solitary, lives in burrows; low metabolic rate; doesn't eat frequently; the female on average lays between 5-18 eggs once every 4 years, the longest reproductive cycle of any reptile
Diet: arthropods, earthworms, snails, bird eggs, small birds, frogs, lizards, weta
Map: species found in New Zealand on 30 small, inaccessible islands off the coast
Habitat: cliffbound
Major Threats: lower risk
Status: Least Concern

THE NOCTURNALS

The information in the glossary was created through research on the IUCN Red List of Threatened Species (http://www.iucnredlist.org/), the University of Michigan's Museum of Zoology Animal Diversity Web (http://animaldiversity.org/) and BirdLife International (http://www.birdlife.org/).

Discussion Questions for Your Book Club

1. Define the word "ominous" and discuss the qualities of mystery, horror and adventure. Does *The Ominous Eye* fit in these genres? What other genres would the novel fit? What genres would it not fit?

2. All story plots contain a conflict, a climax and a resolution. What is the conflict in *The Ominous Eye*, and how is it introduced? What is the climax? The resolution?

3. The members of The Nocturnal Brigade are all different animals. What is the advantage of this? How does Tobin use his long tongue to save Bismark? What characteristics do Dawn and Bismark have and how do they help the Brigade on their adventures? How would the Brigade be different if they were all the same animal?

4. If you were to pick one character from the book who is the most like you, who would it be and why? Who is the most unlike you and why? Which character from the book would you most want as your friend and why?

5. The Nocturnal Brigade wears capes when they set out to solve a mystery. What is the purpose of the capes? Do you think it makes the Brigade more courageous and brave? Can you think of other examples of stories where the characters wear special garments to help them feel brave?

6. How is Dawn the voice of reason within the Brigade? How does the "beast" almost destroy these qualities in her? Does the dangerous situation strengthen or weaken Dawn as a leader throughout the story? How so?

7. Polyphema gains control over the animals. How is she able to do this? Why does she do it? How does each member of the Brigade respond differently to Polyphema's control?

8. How does Polyphema use Otto, the owl, to create further panic? Does her plan work? What role does Otto play in helping the Brigade discover the truth?

9. Who is the real source of the destruction and mayhem in the valley? What clues help you discover that there is no "beast"? How does Dawn discover the real source? How does Dawn deal with Polyphema?

10. Discuss the concept of fear and what role it plays in the story. What do the animals learn about fear from Polyphema's false story? What does Polyphema learn from the Brigade? Can you think of other animal fables with similar lessons?

11. What things in the book would you have done like the Brigade? What things would you have done differently?

12. Discuss the role humor plays in *The Ominous Eye*, both for you as the reader and for the characters. What characters do you find the most humorous? What part did you find the most humorous? How would the book be different without humor?

Q&A with Tracey Hecht

What inspired you to write a middle grade series like
The Nocturnals?

When I put my kids to bed they come up with every excuse
on earth to stay up just a bit later! "I'm hungry." "I need
to go to the bathroom." "I'm not tired!" "I'm thirsty."
Sound familiar? I thought it would be fun to write a book
series for kids that started when their day ended. That way
they could go to sleep thinking of a world that was just
waking up and getting started.

What surprised you the most while writing
The Nocturnals?

How much I like the research! Learning about unusual
animals is one of the most fun things about the series. I love
using the physical traits and unique characteristics of the
animals to help develop characters and enhance plot. The
details I learn about the nocturnal world are constantly
engaging and inspiring me.

**Why did you choose the pangolin, fox, and sugar glider
for your three main characters? Who is your favorite?**

I chose a fox because they're such interesting and cool
animals. A pangolin because they are so unusual and physically captivating. And the sugar glider because…well, that's

a secret! I constantly change my mind in regards to my favorite character, but outside of the brigade, I do love Cora in this book.

Why did you choose the critically endangered pangolin as a main character?

Spend 10 minutes watching YouTube videos or reading about pangolins and you'll understand why I had to have one as a member of the brigade. Everything about the pangolin is fascinating, their physical traits, their behaviors, their appearance. Plus, despite being the most illegally traded animal in the world, very few people know about the pangolin. Hopefully Tobin will help raise awareness for his amazing species.

Why did you choose the endangered tuatara as a main character?

It was a bit like Tobin the pangolin, once I learned about the tuatara, I was instantly captivated. It's the last living species of the order Sphenodontia! But it was the 'third eye' on the top of the tuatara's head that really inspired me. The research of the tuatara led to the idea of *The Ominous Eye* and from there, the plot just followed.

Why did you base the book on Australia?

It's based on Australia? I thought it was a fictitious place!

Most nocturnal animals are from hot, dry places- Africa, Australia, South East Asia, India. We draw from all of them.

Why did you become a writer?

I've always been a writer, since I was young. I was an English/Creative Writing major in college and found jobs even from early on in entertainment and marketing that allowed me to write.   I love to create stories, and even more I love to create characters.

How and when do you write?

I need to carve time and space out of my schedule to write. Quiet, open time and space, and for a sustained period. My ideal writing dynamic is from about 5:30 am until about 10 am at the kitchen table of my house in Maine. Everyone in my family sleeps late so I get to be all alone. As I write, I watch and listen to the day wake up all around me. It's perfection. I do that everyday except for Sundays when I let myself sleep in. I love Sundays too!

Why did you create a three-person protagonist voice with The Nocturnal Brigade?

I have been told that a three-person protagonist voice is unusual for middle grade fiction. The Nocturnals doesn't have a classic narrator voice, or single protagonist point-of-view. The three main characters – Bismark the sugar glider, Tobin the pangolin, and Dawn the fox – all speak together in a 'singular' voice that works in a loose 3-2-1 pattern. That is, for every three words from Bismark, there are two words from Tobin, and one word from Dawn. While this ratio is not literal, it is the guiding rhythm that helps to distinguish the voice of the series.

Bismark is a tiny marsupial who yammers on and on (and on!). Tobin chimes in to frame Bismark's rants, and then Dawn speaks a word or two to punctuate the conversation. It's snappy, cheeky, and from what we have seen, compels a kid to read (and share it) out loud which is our goal.

What is your favorite hobby when you're not writing?

It depends on the season. I like a curled-up-in-front-of-the-fire winter day, a great book, a movie, doing something cozy. I love the summer when I'm in my home in Maine, spending my time outdoors hiking and swimming and cooking over a fire late into the night. One of my favorite things to do is to paddle board on a glassy lake under a sky full of stars. I also adore New York City in the fall—shopping, walking the streets and eating out. My hobbies really do change based on the season.

Acknowledgements

by Sarah Fieber, head writer of The Ominous Eye

First and foremost, to Tracey Hecht: the creator of this series, my boss, and my friend. Thank you so much for giving me the opportunity to do what I love everyday. I can't imagine my career or my world without you.

To Tommy Fagin and Rumur Dowling, my fellow writers. Tommy: thank you for being there from the very beginning, for sticking by me through thick and thin, and for your invaluable edits. Rumur: thank you for your feedback at every odd hour, for making me laugh through the stress and fatigue, and for your incredible help. I couldn't have done this without your friendship and support.

To Susan Lurie, for her rounds of thorough edits (and necessary leveling!). To the wonderful team at Consortium. To Stacey Ashton and everyone at Fabled Films: Lisette Farah, Nicole Wheeler, Waymond Singleton, Nina Passero, Joe Gervasi. Thank you for keeping things running and for making it fun. To Bailey Carr, who animates the words with her readings. To Kate Liebman, who brings the writing to life with her beautiful illustrations.

To everyone outside the office. To Aaron: for your interest, your feedback, and your animal expertise. Without you, there'd be no Tutu! To my unofficial editor, Ryan. To my lifelines: Sam and Savit. To all my incredible friends.

To my family. My brothers: Brian, Greg, and Daniel. My grandparents: Nana and Gramps, Grammy and Poppy. And my parents. Mom, Dad: I write words for a living, but I can't find ones that express what your support means to me. Thank you for everything.

And finally, of course, to Beau: my happiness and inspiration.

Thank you again, everyone.

About the Author

Tracey Hecht is a writer and entrepreneur who has written, directed and produced several films and founded multiple businesses. Her company Fabled Films is releasing The Nocturnals.

About the Illustrator

Kate Liebman is an artist who lives and works in New York City. She graduated from Yale University, contributes to the Brooklyn Rail, and has shown her work at various galleries.

About Fabled Films

Fabled Films is a publishing and entertainment company creating original content for middle grade and YA audiences. Fabled Films Press combines strong literary properties with high quality production values to connect books with generations of parents and their children. Each property is supported with additional content in the form of animated web series and social media as well as websites featuring activities for children, parents, bookstores, educators and librarians.

FABLED FILMS PRESS
NEW YORK CITY

www.fabledfilms.com

The Adventures Continue in Book 3 of The Nocturnals

Visit nocturnalsworld.com
to watch animated videos, download fun nighttime
activities and check out a map of the Brigade's
adventure at nocturnalsworld.com/map/

*

Teachers and Librarians get Common Core Language Arts and
Next Generation Science guides for the book series.

*

#NocturnalsWorld